It doesn't matter how far you run...

THE *Dirty Heroes* COLLECTION

HUNTED

CASSANDRA FAYE

Text copyright © 2020 Cassandra Faye
All Rights Reserved

No part of this book may be reproduced in any form or by any electronic or mechanical means including information storage and retrieval systems, without permission in writing from the author. The only exception is by a reviewer, who may quote short excerpts in a review.

This book is a work of fiction. Names, characters, places, and incidents either are products of the author's imagination or are used fictitiously. Any resemblance to actual persons, living or dead, events, or locales is entirely coincidental.

ISBN (e-book): 978-1-946722-56-0
ISBN (paperback): 978-1-946722-57-7

Cover design by Jay Aheer, www.simplydefinedart.com
Formatting by Raven Designs

The Dirty Heroes
COLLECTION

The Black Fox, by Brianna Hale

Finding His Strength, by Measha Stone

While She Sleeps, by Dani René

Bound by Sacrifice, by Murphy Wallace

Never Lost, by TL Mayhew

The Curse Behind The Mask, by Holly J. Gill

Clockwork Stalker, by Cari Silverwood

Kiss and Tell, by Jo-Anne Joseph

Skeleton King, by Charity B.

Make Me Real, by Petra J. Knox

Cruel Water, by Dee Palmer

The Masked Prince, by Faith Ryan

Hunted, by Cassandra Faye

The Lady, by Golden Angel

BLURB

> "It doesn't matter how far she runs.
> This is my forest, and I always catch my prey."

As a Loxley, I know the rules,
I just never took them seriously.
I only knew when I finally brought a girl here
it would be special.
She would be special.
And Harper is... perfect.

Now we're out here, alone,
and something's gone terribly wrong.
I broke the rules, I'm losing myself,
and I'm afraid she's going to pay the price.

I need to fight this. I need to protect Harper.
We're meant to be, and I know she feels the same.
I don't want to hurt her but... I have to claim her.
I have to make her mine.
Before I do something I can't take back.

Dedication

Thank you, Katie, for always loving my words, no matter how crazy they get, and thank you Niki for helping me stay upright even when I insist on falling down again and again.

Finally, thank you to Gabriela for taking my words to the next level, and always being a bright light in the dark. I love you guys.

Once upon a time, a scorned Queen opened a box, unleashing horrible evil on the world's heroes.

Instead of gallantry and chivalry, they now possessed much more perverse traits. They've fallen victim to their darkest and most deviant desires.

This is one of their stories...

CHAPTER ONE
Harper

"How much farther, babe?" Twisting in my seat, I lean against the door to watch Jared as he drives, one hand holding onto the steering wheel.

"Maybe fifteen or twenty minutes," he answers, looking at me for a quick second as a grin spreads over his lips. "Depends on if any trees are down, or if the road got washed out near the creek. If there are any issues, you might have to get your hands dirty, Ms. Bainbridge."

Laughing, I lean forward to smack his arm. "Since when do I avoid getting my hands dirty, *Mr. Loxley*?"

"Oh, I know you like it dirty, even though you're a Bainbridge of the Connecticut

Bainbridges," he says, using his *Lifestyles of the Rich and Famous* voice. Glancing at me again, Jared's eyebrows dance up and down until I roll my eyes and point out the windshield.

"You're such a dumbass. Would you just watch the road, so you don't kill us on the way to your *mysterious* cabin?" I wiggle my fingers in the air, using a spooky voice to mock him for the hundredth time for treating the cabin like some epic secret.

"Trust me, Harper, it's worth the wait. And, come on, you know you love me," he replies, the grin lingering on his face as he props an elbow on the open window, green eyes returning to the rough dirt road winding through the trees.

"You're lucky I love you so much," I answer, smiling as I watch him laugh before he reaches over to squeeze my hand.

"I'm incredibly lucky." Jared winks at me, and I feel the same rush of warm, bubbly energy that I felt the first time he did. Sophomore year at Dartmouth, in an intro to philosophy course. It had been a big room, but the seats were already filling up by the time I made it inside. Jared was sitting by one of his friends near the back row, and he'd looked back at the door as I searched for an empty seat when our gazes had locked like a scene out of some movie. I'd thought he was cute, but when that smile spread across his lips, lighting up his entire face, he'd instantly changed from cute to *hot* — and then he'd winked at me. I didn't know it at the time, but I was already lost to him, and when he tilted his head at the empty seat beside him, I didn't even hesitate.

That was two years ago and falling in love with Jared Loxley is the easiest thing I've ever done. He's perfect, to me anyway. Charming, hilarious, and somehow both an absolute gentleman and the dirtiest joker ever. I love that he never underestimates me, that he's never hesitated to take me on these outdoor adventures he loves so much, and while I did grow up in a nice family, I've fallen in love with the outdoors too. Hiking, camping, kayaking, rock climbing — he's taught me to do all of it. Always patient, always watching out for me. He's easy to love.

Of course, as my friends always remind me, it doesn't hurt that he's hot as hell.

The air smells sweet as we continue on, and I lean my head back out the window, looking up at the perfect blue sky framed by the trees that huddle close to what serves as the road into his family's property. The same property that apparently has no address, just a set of longitude and latitude coordinates guiding us, along with his years of experience coming out here to find the muddy track leading in and out.

I may not know why Jared and his family keep the cabin such a secret, but I know we're going to have a blast this weekend — it's impossible not to have fun around him.

"Oh good, the bridge still looks solid," Jared says, half to himself, but I sit up straight, a nervous laugh bubbling up and past my lips.

"Was there a *question* about the safety of the bridge?" I ask, trying to hold onto the laugh as I look out the windshield at the wooden structure spanning the creek.

"Dad was out here about a month ago with Ollie and he said it was fine, but there's been a few storms up here since then. The creek looks calm, but it's deeper than you think, and it can get wild when the rains come down the mountains." Reaching over, Jared pats my knee, smiling at me as he starts to move the SUV across. "I promise you're safe, babe."

The creaking of the wood under us seems to be questioning him, but I force myself to look at him again and smile. "I trust you."

"Good," he answers, squeezing my knee just before he lifts his hands in the air and claps them together. "Aaaand we're across! See? We didn't die. Perfectly safe."

"Would we have figured out that it wasn't safe before or *after* the car went into the water?" I ask, and he laughs.

"Probably before?" Tilting his head, he pretends to think hard, and I groan as he continues. "Definitely during the fall into the water, but you know I'd rescue you. I'm the king of the outdoors, remember?"

"I don't remember 'bridge construction' being a part of your skill set as king of the outdoors."

"It's definitely in there." Nodding, Jared lets out another laugh as the SUV bounces over a few rough dips on the road. "I'm just going to have to update my kingly resumé."

"Riiiight." Shaking my head, I can't help but laugh along with him. I gave him the 'king of the outdoors' title on our first camping trip when he'd impressed me with his skills setting up camp and cooking for us. It was like he'd been born in the woods, like he belonged there, and so for his birthday that year I'd bought him a shirt with the title printed on it, and he loved it. It's got holes in it now, but he still wears it all the time, and I'd bet a hundred bucks he's got it packed for this trip.

Jared starts humming to himself, tapping his thumb on the steering wheel to the rhythm of whatever song is playing in his head. Leaning against the door again, I look off into the trees, loving the way the sunlight changes the color of the leaves from bright, pale green at the top to dusky and dull closer to the forest floor. I can see why he loves this place so much… it's beautiful.

"So how much of this is your property?"

"We've got a little over two hundred acres, and the cabin is tucked almost in the middle of it," he answers, and I try to remember what the hell that means in normal language.

"That sounds like a lot," I reply lamely, and

he chuckles.

"Yeah, it's one of the bigger properties up here, but my family grabbed it forever ago. I think my great-great-grandfather built the first cabin, and the family just keeps improving it." Leaning forward, he points through the windshield at one of the rolling mountains. "That's Mitchell Mountain. It's got an open summit and when we're up there you'll be able to see all the way to Lake Champlain. Luckily, our cabin is higher up than a lot of the others, which gives us some great views anyway, and there's always a ton of deer."

"Is that dinner?" I ask, even though I already know the answer.

Jared smacks his chest with his fist, rolling his shoulders back as he lets out a grunt. "Me king of outdoors. Me feed my woman."

"I've got Tarzan for a boyfriend, I'm so lucky!" Laughing, I grab the water bottle and take a drink as he winks at me again. "At least I know you'd help me survive a zombie apocalypse."

"Oh yeah, we'd totally survive. And, for the record, I promise I won't make you clean the deer," Jared says as he shifts in his seat, twisting to stretch out his back. We've been driving for hours, and I'm sure he's as ready as I am to get the fuck out of the car. Just thinking about it makes me stretch my legs out, arching my back against the seat to loosen my stiff muscles.

Aaaand now I have to pee. Awesome.

"Please tell me this super secret cabin has a bathroom." Putting the water bottle back into the cupholder, I try to ignore the suddenly insistent nudge from my bladder.

"Of course it does," he replies, chuckling. "I told you we've updated it. There's indoor plumbing, well water, a septic system, and *electricity*."

"Ooooo, so fancy!" I joke, trying to find a comfortable position, but it's not working. It's like now that I'm aware of my need to pee, it's all my body can focus on. "Well, are we close? Because if we're not then I'm going to need you to stop so I can visit a tree."

"Five more minutes, babe. Can you hold it?" Jared asks, but I can tell he's not teasing me. He'll stop the car if I ask him to, but I'd much prefer a real toilet than risking squatting in the wrong place.

"I'm good." I smile at him and he reaches over to hold my hand, lacing our fingers together. Jared may be a joker, and rarely serious, but he always takes care of me and I love him even more for it.

It takes seven minutes, not five, before the cabin comes into view, and there were a few moments as the SUV bounced along the road that I thought about giving up on the thought of indoor plumbing — but I'm glad I didn't. I don't know what I expected from the Loxley's top-secret hideaway, but the one-story log cabin looks a lot nicer than whatever I'd been picturing in the back of my mind. It's clear from the different tones in the wood where sections have been added on, but it somehow works, looking both rustic and modern at the same time.

"Doesn't this count as 'glamping?'" I ask, knowing how much he hates the concept, but he just laughs.

"Probably, but it's tradition." Pulling the car to a stop near the door, he turns it off and jingles the keys as he pulls them free. "Come on, babe.

I'll let you inside to use the bathroom before I turn on the generator and everything."

"Thank God," I reply, climbing out of the car as my bladder threatens a full mutiny. It's my own fault though. If I hadn't ordered the spicy sandwich at the deli in town, I wouldn't have chugged my entire water bottle — and half of Jared's — on the drive up here.

The inside of the cabin is definitely a man cave, but I don't have long to look around the living room before Jared shows me the bathroom. I did notice the deer heads and antlers adorning the wall above the fireplace though, and although I've never been against the idea of hunting, the trophies sort of creep me out. I think it's the eyes, or the marbles, or whatever they put in their heads. They're just… empty. Shiny, black orbs that seem to follow me wherever I am.

Shaking off the shiver that rolls up my back, I use the toilet and then move to the sink. The pipes groan when I turn the water faucet on and water sputters from the spout a few times before the flow picks up, but I'm relieved the guys at least have hand soap here. The loud *clunk* of the generator kicking on has me reaching over to flip the light switch as I dry my hands on the towel. It takes a second, but yellow bulbs come to life above the mirror and I smile at my reflection.

"Running water and electricity? This is *definitely* not Jared's usual outdoor adventure," I mutter to myself. Normally, we 'rough it' when we go away for a long weekend. Hiking out with all of our gear to set up camp in some obscure spot Jared heard about from a friend of a friend, but this cabin is more than a step above that. It could easily be someone's home.

"Everything good, babe?" Jared's voice comes through the door and I snap out of my thoughts.

"Yeah! Just putting my hair back up, one sec." Yanking out the hairband from my rumpled ponytail, I quickly finger-comb my hair and pull it into a loose bun to keep it off my neck. When I open the door, Jared isn't there, so I head outside to find him unloading the back of the car.

"Well, what do you think?" he asks, setting my duffel bag beside his on the ground.

"It's really nice. I think I was expecting something more along the lines of pioneer days, not… vacation rental cabin." Shrugging, I grab both of our bags to take them inside as he lifts the large cooler.

"Well, I think it used to be closer to that," Jared says, the muscles in his arms bulging against the fabric of his sleeves as he hauls the heavy cooler toward the door. "But each generation makes it just a little better than before."

"What are you going to add to it?" I ask as I drop one of the duffel bags to hold the door open for him.

"Thanks, babe." Huffing, he moves carefully up the steps to slide sideways through the door, heading for the kitchen as he talks to me over his shoulder. "I'm not sure what Ollie and I will add to it. We'll figure it out when he's older."

"Addison doesn't get to help?" I ask, leaving the duffels by the large leather couch before I follow him into the kitchen. It's narrow, galley-style, but it has a real stove and oven, a fridge, and even a microwave.

Jared shrugs before rolling his shoulders,

stretching his arms out. "Addison hasn't ever been out here."

"Too young?"

"Nah, it's just..." Chuckling, he runs a hand through his hair before he walks past me toward the door. "I guess it sounds sexist when I say it out loud, but none of the women in our family ever come out here."

"That definitely sounds sexist," I reply as we head outside to bring in more of the supplies for the long weekend.

"Well, I think it's just tradition at this point. I mean, Dad brought me out here for the first time when I was eight or nine. Oliver came with us when he turned nine, but Addison is fifteen and he's never even talked about it." Blowing out a breath, Jared stops beside the car and turns to look at me. "You're right, it's totally sexist."

"Yep," I say, letting my lips pop at the end of the word, and he reaches over to pull me against him, his arms wrapping around the small of my back.

"*I'm* not sexist though."

"So, you'd bring your daughter out here?" The question hovers between us when he doesn't immediately answer, and I feel a buzz rush down my spine as Jared's gaze slides down to my lips.

"If she were anything like you… absolutely." Leaning down, he captures my mouth in a kiss that has my skin on fire in seconds. Nipping my lip, he deepens the kiss with a flick of his tongue, pulling me harder against his firm chest, and I know little moans are escaping under my breath as I try to tug him closer even though there's not a whisper of air between us.

"Jared…" His name comes out on a sigh as he trails his lips down my neck, finding that thrilling spot by my collarbone that always turns me into a warm puddle of need.

"I love it when you say my name like that," he growls against my skin, nipping my shoulder, and I smile up at the clouds floating overhead as tingles scatter out from the point.

"Jared." I do my best to use the same tone as I say his name again, a quiet moan following on its heels as the steadily hardening bulge in his jeans presses against me.

"Fuck it, we can unload the rest later," he says just before he leans down and throws me over his shoulder.

"Holy shit!" I cry out, cackling as the world flips upside down and Jared turns to head back inside.

"The king of the outdoors must claim his woman!" he shouts as loud as he can, the woods swallowing the sound of his call and my laughter.

CHAPTER TWO
Harper

THE LIVING ROOM SPINS WHEN HE FLIPS ME OFF his shoulder and onto the couch, his hands immediately moving to the button on my shorts.

"How did I get so lucky to snag you?" he whispers, almost inaudible, and I grin as he slips his fingers underneath the waistband of both my shorts and underwear to pull them down in one swoop.

"I say the same thing all the time." The words barely get past my lips before he's kissing me again, hands wrapped around the back of my head, and I cling to his shirt as I toe my shoes off and kick my clothes free. Breaking the kiss, I tug at his shirt. "Off."

"Are you trying to get me naked, Ms. Bainbridge?" he asks, faking shock, and I shove at his hard stomach. Laughing, he stands up to pull it over his head, and I can't help but stare at the way his skin moves and stretches over his muscles. He's not some weird body builder with bulging, lumpy muscles, but he's got broad shoulders and a hint of abs that lead down to the most delicious 'V' just above his jeans. If I didn't want him on top of me so bad, I'd make him switch places with me just so I could lick every inch of him, all the way down to... *that*.

"Please tell me you know where the condoms are," I say with a slight whine in my voice as he drops his jeans, the hard-on tenting his boxers.

"I'll find them, you get naked." Winking at me, Jared moves to the end of the couch, kicking off his jeans before he crouches beside the duffel bags and rips the zipper open. I don't waste any time tossing my bra over the back of the couch, followed by my socks. A second later he stands up, a triumphant grin on his face and a foil packet in his fingers. "Got it."

"Come here." I reach for him, but he doesn't

take my hand. Instead, Jared grabs my legs, hooking his hands behind my knees to push me up the couch before he spreads them and leans in to trace his tongue through my folds. Digging my fingers into the leather cushion, I lift my hips on a gasp. "Oh fuck, Jared…"

"God, I love the way you taste," he groans, delving his tongue in before he drags it up to flick my clit. When he focuses on that little bundle of nerves, my back arches off the couch, but he shifts his hands to my hips to pull me back down, holding me exactly where he wants me so he can drive me crazy. It's intense, a constant stream of thrumming pleasure that has me whining and moaning and murmuring things I can't even make sense of as he builds me higher and higher. A lot of guys treat oral like a chore, but Jared has always loved it, insisted on it. Hell, there's been nights he's camped out between my thighs until I begged him to stop because I was too sensitive to handle another lick.

"Fuck, fuck, fuck!" I cry out when he plunges two fingers inside, curving them to hit my g-spot with a kind of mythological accuracy that has only got better the longer we've been together. His quiet chuckle has me looking down to find him grinning up at me from between my thighs. "What?"

"Nothing, I'm just enjoying the show," he answers just before he captures my clit again, torturing me with merciless pleasure as he sucks and teases me with his tongue.

"Oh God, yes, yes," I whine, panting as my heartrate skyrockets. I can feel the orgasm creeping up on me, like a low buzz in my veins that's steadily getting louder, making my muscles tighter with every squirming shift of my hips as I both try to escape his insistent focus and press myself closer. But just as that perfect oblivion feels like it's about to crash over me, he pulls his fingers free and sits up on the end of the couch. All I can do is whimper, looking up at him as he strokes his cock slowly.

"I'm not going to last long, babe. I've wanted you all fucking day."

Nodding, I reach for him, needing to feel him against me, inside me. "I don't care, I want you."

"Hell yes," he growls, shifting between my

thighs as he grabs the condom off the coffee table and rips it open. When he starts to roll it on, I wrap my hand around his, squeezing as he glides his hand down, and I love the way his eyes close, jaw tight as he groans low. "Fuck, Harper…"

"Exactly," I reply, grinning at him when he opens them again.

"You want me inside you?" he asks, a wicked smile spreading over his lips as he leans down, lining up his cock only to slide outside of me, stroking his hard shaft over my clit.

"Don't tease me," I whine, looking up into his green eyes that seem so much darker with the way his pupils have dilated, but he just rocks his hips, the latex gliding through the wet mess between my thighs.

"I want to hear you say it, Harper. Tell me how much you want me to fuck you until you come around my cock," he whispers right against my ear, his teeth grazing my skin as he groans, and I can feel the rumble of it in his chest as he presses me into the cushions. "Tell me you want me to make this sweet little pussy mine."

"Fuck! Please, Jared! I need you. I want you

to fuck me. I'll say whatever you want just *please* stop teasing me." His self-control is something that drives me insane, and he knows it. It's why he likes to drag it out, to go down on me until I'm writhing and needy, tempting me until I'm desperate and soaked and ready for him.

"God, I love you," he growls as he shifts his hips back and then presses against my entrance, moving inside slowly as he stretches me. Our groans echo in unison, and my nails find his back, digging in as I feel the incredible aching bliss of him filling me. Jared isn't the longest guy I've been with, but he's so fucking thick that the first time we had sex was a lesson in patience and I was sore for days.

Maybe that's why he's got such ridiculous self-control.

"You can do it," I whisper, biting down on the moan as I lift my hips to pull him deeper. "I'm okay."

"You sure?" He kisses me, teasing me with a flick of his tongue before he looks down at me, waiting. All I can manage is a nod in response, and he licks and kisses his way down my throat until he finds that spot by my collarbone that has my whole body tingling just before he thrusts hard. There's a flicker of pain, but I'm more than ready for him and when he pulls back and drives in again, there's only pleasure. Growling against my shoulder, he starts to pick up the pace. "Fuck, Harper. The sounds you make…"

"More," I beg, unable to form a full sentence as he starts to really fuck me. He's strong, fit from all his time outdoors and playing baseball at school, and every inch of muscle in his body makes each thrust count. It doesn't take long before I'm hovering on the edge of that perfect oblivion again, the tension inside reaching critical levels, and all I can do is lift my hips to meet his with loud claps of skin, the sound of it blending with our moans and rough breaths as we seek our bliss in each other.

"Harper…" He growls my name, teeth capturing that place on my shoulder that has me crying out, and I know he's telling me he can't hold out much longer — but it doesn't matter. Between one breath and the next the world flips upside down, my head spinning with a chaotic maelstrom of electrical signals that choke off my cry with pure ecstasy. I come so hard that for a moment it's like the universe blinks out of existence, shattering with the force of the orgasm, and when I'm finally able to breathe again my awareness returns to the incredible feeling of his cock driving as deep as he can go. So good, so perfectly full. Jared whispers my name again as he comes, jerking inside me, and there's other words in the murmurs against my skin but I don't catch them. My ears are still buzzing from the aftershocks, muscles trembling as his weight presses me into the couch, comforting me as we both try to catch our breath.

"I love you so fucking much." The words come out in huffs, but I feel him chuckling before he props himself up on his elbow.

"Is that the orgasm talking?" he asks, grinning, and I squeeze him inside me, watching his eyes flutter closed as he groans. "Fuck… you're going to kill me."

"Why would I do that when you're so damn handy to have around?" My laugh gets cut off when he kisses me, and I'm so overwhelmed by the feeling of happiness that I lose whatever smart-ass thing I was going to say next.

"I hope you always feel that way, babe,"

he whispers, his nose brushing mine before he kisses me again, and I just hug him against me since I can't answer. These kisses are sweeter, softer, and it's just one more reason that I love him. He slides from me as he shifts back, and I already miss the feeling of fullness, of his skin against mine. "I'll be right back."

Sitting up on the couch, I watch as he heads toward the bathroom, and I chew on my thumbnail as I admire his backside. Jared is definitely hot, even more so now that we're heading into our senior year than he was when we first met, but it's like he doesn't know it — which, I guess, is a good thing. He wouldn't be so attractive if he was just another cocky frat boy who thinks he's God's gift to women, but sometimes I wonder if he won't wake up and realize just how amazing he is and go find someone else.

Shut up, shut up, shut up.

I don't know what it is about my brain that's always waiting for the other shoe to drop. I've had this nagging feeling like I'm going to screw things up with Jared, or that something else will happen and he'll leave, because why would it make sense for things to be so… perfect?

"You have your thinking face on," he says as he walks back into the living room, and I flash a smile as he moves around the couch to sit beside me.

"I think that's called post-orgasmic catatonia." Cuddling up against him, he wraps his arm around me as he chuckles.

"Gotcha. I think I'm feeling a bit of that as well." Jared presses a kiss to my hair, and I look up at all of the creepy trophies on the wall. All those dead eyes that just watched us have sex.

"Please tell me there's a bed here, because I don't feel like giving the deer another show."

"You don't like them?" Jared leans back a little and I sit up, shrugging as I gesture at the various deer heads above the fireplace, extending to the walls on either side.

"They're creepy as hell. Weird, empty eyes." A shiver runs down my spine and Jared tugs me closer to him.

"Don't worry, there's actually two bedrooms. We just have to put the sheets on." He pokes me in the ribs, waggling his eyebrows at me when I look up at him. "No spooky deer heads to watch me fuck you later."

"Oh, that's happening again?"

"Absolutely. I've got to make up for that performance," he replies, donning a serious expression. "One orgasm? And I didn't last near long enough."

"I enjoyed it a lot," I reply, nudging him with my elbow and he leans down to give me a quick kiss.

"I did too, babe, but you know how much I love to hear you beg me to come."

"There's only so many times a girl can come before it starts to be more pain than pleasure!" Laughing, I shove him a little harder when he shrugs his shoulders like he doesn't believe me. "Seriously, Jared. I'm not going to be able to hike tomorrow if you fuck me for hours tonight."

"Challenge accepted!" he announces, pumping a fist in the air like he's actually planning on it… which isn't impossible. He's done it before.

"Challenge *not* accepted," I say, rolling my eyes. "I thought you wanted to show me the mountain?"

"Oh, you'll be fine." Jared's grin turns

wicked and I nudge him a little harder with my elbow.

"You're so bad."

"I think you meant *good*. I'm so *good* at fucking you until you can't walk because I'm a good boyfriend," he replies.

"Well, that, but I think it has a little more to do with how *not* little you are." I drop my gaze to his dick and his smile gets even bigger.

"Hold on, I need to record that." Jared starts to get up, and I catch his arm and pull him back, laughing as he drops onto the couch beside me.

"No way!"

"Oh, come on, that's like… the number one thing every guy wants to hear. I want to be able to play it on repeat, or, better yet, have it as my alarm in the mornings." He tries to give me puppy dog eyes, but I just shove him playfully and roll mine again.

"Not happening, babe. I love you though."

"I love you, too," he says before pulling me against him.

I'm way too comfortable snuggled into the warmth of his chest with his arm draped across my back, but then I remember the rest of the stuff in the SUV. "Shit, did you close the back of the car? Or roll up the windows?"

Jared's chest shakes a little as he laughs. "No, but I'm sure the family of squirrels that have taken up residence will appreciate our forethought in bringing so much trail mix."

"Oh my God, Jared! We need to get it closed up," I say, trying to stand up, but he holds on tight.

"Five more minutes isn't going to mean anything," he replies, tucking me into his side. "Plus, we probably shouldn't bother the bears until they're done going through everything."

"Please tell me you're joking." I tilt my head up, trying to get a good look at his face, but it's not necessary because he cracks in seconds, his laughter rolling out.

"It's fine, babe. I promise. No bears." He traces a pattern on my thigh with his free hand, falling silent for a minute until I hear him chuckling softly again. "Well, there *are* bears around here, but we probably won't see one. They tend to avoid people. I always carry a gun just in case though."

"That is absolutely not comforting."

"Well, then I probably shouldn't remind you that moose are infinitely more dangerous?" he adds, and I reach over to smack his chest. "Ouch! So mean!"

"I didn't hurt you," I reply, sighing as I try to shake off the frisson of anxiety. It's not like there isn't always a risk of running into something when we're out camping, but that's usually in a national park where there are rangers, and places close by to get help. Out here? There's nothing.

Awesome.

"Don't worry about it. All the times my dad and I have been out here, we've maybe seen bears twice, and they avoided us. You don't need to worry." Jared reaches for my hand, interlacing our fingers, but I'm not worrying about bears anymore.

"Hey… is your dad going to be upset that you brought me out here?"

I feel him stiffen, and his silence is suddenly deafening.

"Jared?" Pushing away from him, I sit up on the couch to see if he's joking with me again but this time the serious, thoughtful look on his

face is real.
Well, fuck.

CHAPTER THREE
Jared

"Why would you think he'd be upset?" I ask, trying to avoid the topic, but I should know better. Harper doesn't drop anything if she thinks there's a secret.

"Earlier you said he doesn't bring any of the women in the family here."

Shit.

"Well, he used to bring my mom before I was born." Standing up from the couch, I grab my boxer-briefs from the floor and pull them on. "It's not a big deal, babe. Okay?"

"Have you ever brought anyone else here?" she asks, and I want to groan. If she keeps digging, she's going to figure it out, and I can't risk that. I have *plans*.

"No, but I haven't ever dated a girl that actually liked doing the outdoorsy stuff with me. They just faked it until the first time they had to pee in the woods or had to go two days without a real shower." I grab my jeans and continue getting dressed, but Harper isn't even moving… which means she's not going to give up.

"What about friends?"

Fuck, fuck, fuck.

"Nah, this has always been more a family thing. Me and Dad, you know?" I answer, pulling my shirt on over my head as I walk around the couch to grab her bra and socks from the floor. When I hand them to her, she's got that look on her face she gets whenever we're watching some murder show and she's trying to figure out who did it.

But this is one case Detective Harper isn't going to be allowed to crack, even if I have to literally run away from her.

"So, I'm the first person you've brought here?" She's got a smile on her face, a faint blush in her cheeks, and I give her my most charming smile as I pick up her underwear and her shorts, spinning the underwear on my finger.

"You're the only one I've had sex with here, that's for damn sure." Laughing, I toss them onto the couch and turn toward the door. "I'm going to check on the car and finish unloading, you can join me once you're able to walk again."

"Jared, wait!"

Please drop it, Harper. Please.

Stopping at the door, I turn to look at her, trying to hold onto the smile and not look like my heart is trying to pound out of my chest. "What's up, babe?"

"We're not supposed to be here, are we," she says, and it's definitely not a question.

"Well…"

"I knew it! *This* is why you've been so weird about this trip! And why you wouldn't let me mention anything about a camping trip or a cabin or the Adirondacks on Facebook or Instagram or anything." Groaning, Harper buries her face in her shirt, and I feel like the floor is slowly slipping out from underneath me. "Your dad is going to fucking hate me if he finds out about this."

Thank God.

"First of all, he's not going to find out. He thinks I'm out here solo doing some hiking and hunting to stock our freezer. Second, he would never hate you. Hell, I'm pretty sure he likes you more than me." Clapping my hands together, I tilt my head toward the door. "Trust me, it's fine. I'll bring in the rest of the stuff, okay?"

"If you say so. I think I'm going to change into jeans, it's cooler up here than I thought." Harper stands up to pull on her underwear, and then I see her moving toward the duffel bags. Toward *my* duffel bag... which is still open from when I dug out the condoms.

"Wait!" Rushing over, I grab my bag from the floor and gesture toward the larger bedroom. "Let me show you which room we'll use."

"Uh, okaaaay. You're acting really strange, Jared. What's up?" Harper gives me a weird look and I force a quick laugh before pointing at the deer heads.

"I thought you didn't want an audience?"

Rolling her eyes, she scoops up her bag. "Good point. I can go ahead and get the sheets on the bed too."

"Sounds like a plan," I answer, taking a

deep breath to try and slow my racing heart.

Fuck me. I've got to chill out or I'm going to give everything away.

An hour later, and the fridge has finally chilled enough to move stuff from the cooler, which means we'll be completely unpacked and ready to enjoy the weekend.

"Here, babe." I hand her the milk, and she puts it away, turning around to accept the yogurt I've already got waiting for her. Sitting on the floor of the kitchen by the cooler, our tiny version of a bucket brigade means we'll be done soon, which means I can distract her with something else. Maybe a quick hike. As I hand off the rest of her yogurt, my eyes drift to the bedroom we'll be in tonight.

It's the one Dad has always slept in, which makes me feel kind of weird, but it has the bigger bed. It wouldn't exactly be a romantic weekend for us to cram onto one of the twin beds in the smaller room, and there's no way in hell I'm sleeping in a separate bed just to stay out of 'Dad's room.' Before we moved in together, I slept like shit on the nights she stayed at her place, and even though both of our parents weren't fans of us getting an apartment together... it seems like we've weathered the worst of that.

Pretty much.

Staring at the door has me rethinking where I left my duffel bag. I debated tossing it in the closet, but that would have just made her curious enough to look inside it, so I'd left it against the wall on my side of the bed instead — which means it should be safe. Probably. At least I was able to rearrange my bag while Harper was changing so that even if she does look for something in it, it isn't likely she'll stumble across the only secret I'm *actually* keeping from her.

Everything leading up to this trip has had me in knots. I hadn't meant to keep the cabin itself a secret, but when I'd told her it didn't have an address, she'd started teasing me about my family having a secret compound 'off the grid.' But while this place is definitely off the grid, it's not exactly a secret, it's just...

for family. Regardless, the secrecy of the cabin kept Harper busy for the last few weeks, which meant she wasn't digging into other things that would have ruined our whole weekend.

The likelihood that Dad could find out about her being here is pretty low, and if she mentions it to him years from now it won't even matter.

"So, what are we doing for dinner tonight, oh king of the outdoors?" Harper asks, looking down at me with her hands on her hips and the fridge door closed. I've been so distracted by my thoughts, that I didn't even realize I'd handed her the last items.

Shaking off the haze in my brain, I flip the lid of the cooler closed again and push myself up from the floor. "Unfortunately, tonight is probably going to be sandwiches. I'll head out early in the morning to try and grab us a deer."

"How early?" She gives me a look that says my reply of 'dawn' isn't going to be a welcome one, and I chuckle.

"You don't need to come with me, babe. I'll sneak out and hopefully have one hung up in the cellar before you're up and about."

"That's not fair, Jared. I'll come with—"

"It's fine, babe. I promise. I know you don't like to watch me kill something," I say as I pull her against me, leaning down to breathe in the scent of her shampoo. "Even if you do enjoy the results."

"And what results are those?" she asks, tilting her head to the side so I can run my lips down her neck, dragging my tongue over the edge of her collarbone.

"Good food," I whisper, nipping her skin just so I can hear that sweet little gasp she makes. "A boyfriend who is a total manly man."

"Manly man?" she repeats on a laugh, and I can't help but grin as I lift my head to capture her mouth in a kiss.

"I'm super manly." Adding a caveman grunt to the end has her laughing, her bright smile lighting up her whole face, and I have to remind myself that I can't rush the plan for the weekend. I love her so damn much, and I just have to hope she feels the same.

"My king of the outdoors." Harper kisses me and I pull her closer, wrapping my arms around her back as we taste each other, neither of us pushing for anything more than just *this*.

She's perfect. So damn down to earth, so fun, and I have no idea how she ended up this way when her family is the stereotypical uptight, traditional, rich asshats. More obsessed with their name and social standing than anything as real as the earth under their feet.

But Harper is different. She's kind, open-minded, and up for anything.

Breaking the kiss, she smiles up at me, her warm brown eyes searching mine. "Okay, king, what's the plan for the evening?"

"Up to you, babe. We can go for a quick hike before we lose the light, or we could save our energy for the hike tomorrow and just stay in."

"Will you show me around your secret cabin?" she asks, grinning at me with a mischievous expression.

"You've pretty much seen the entire thing. It's not very big."

"Come on, show me around." Harper grabs my hand, pulling me into the living room with her as she walks backward. "What did your dad add to the cabin? What makes it so secret and special? What do you guys normally do out here?"

Sighing, I point at the door to the room we'll be sleeping in. "That's the room dad usually sleeps in, and Ollie and I always slept in this one." Intertwining our fingers, I tug her over to the small bedroom beside the bathroom and open the door. The twin beds are bare, pushed against opposite walls, and an old, scarred desk is tucked under the window.

"It's so bare," she says, letting go of my hand to walk further in.

"What did you expect? Posters of boy bands?" Leaning against the doorframe, I chuckle when she shoots a look at me. "Hey, don't judge me for my love of One Direction."

"Oh, really? Who was your favorite? Harry, Zayn?"

"I'm definitely a Zayn Malik fan," I answer, and she laughs.

"Oh my God, are you being serious?" Harper asks, and I shrug, holding a straight face for about ten seconds before I crack.

"It's not my thing, but Addison was obsessed so I know more than I probably should about One Direction and all the drama involved." Chuckling, I point at the desk. "Ollie and I carved our initials underneath that. I don't know if Dad has ever noticed."

"Really?" Crouching down, she looks under it, reaching up to trace her fingers across the wood, and I'm distracted by her curves again. "This is cool. It'll probably be here for generations."

"That's the plan anyway," I reply, shrugging a little as I remember sitting underneath it beside Ollie as we carved out the letters with our pocketknives, adding the year for good measure. "That desk has been here since before I was born for sure."

"I love it." Standing up, she peeks out the window, and the warm gold of the setting sun turns strands of her brown hair into fire. "This place is really beautiful."

"Thanks." Gesturing back into the living room, I beckon her. "Come on, let me show you the rest."

"How long would you guys normally spend out here?" she asks as she follows me.

"Usually a week, sometimes a long weekend. This is the mud room." Opening the door to the small space, I point at the large sink and the plastic mat on the floor in front of it. "This is where we wash up from outside, so we don't track too much shit inside the house."

"Cool."

"And this is what my dad added to the house," I say as I ignore the backdoor and punch in the code to the locked room to open it for Harper. Flicking on the light, I move aside so she can see inside. Her eyes go wide, but she walks in after a moment and I'm curious about how she's going to react.

"This is… a lot of weapons."

"Yeah." The long, narrow room extends all the way to the edge of the cabin, but there's no windows so that if someone were to wander onto our land and find it, they wouldn't be able to see the real treasures of the place. "My family have always been hunters, and that means we've collected quite a few things."

"I thought the ones you had at home were the only ones you had," she mumbles, and I hate that I can't tell how she feels.

"Well, kind of. Those are mine, but these belong to the family. Some of this shit is so old we couldn't use it anyway, but we keep it because they're basically heirlooms." Moving inside I stop beside her where she's staring at one of the bows. "You can touch them. You're not going to hurt anything."

"Where's the string?" Harper asks, running her fingers along the wood of a recurve bow on a rack.

"Can't leave it strung or it'll weaken the wood. If we want to use it, we have to restring it before we go out. Want me to show you how?" I pick up the one she's looking at, but she shakes her head.

"I'm good. I've just never seen this many guns or bows in one place."

Chuckling, I look around the room and I have to agree with her. The left wall is covered in wooden dowels to support all the bows, and the right has racks of rifles and two handmade units underneath with drawers. Inside those are handguns, ammo, string, and a lot of knives. "I guess it does look like we could open a store or something, but it's generations of stuff. A lot of it used to be in the cellar, but Dad wanted to keep it more secure and store everything the right way. Keep it in good shape, you know?"

"That makes sense." Turning around, her eyes linger on the rifles before skirting the cabinets. "So, you know how to use all this?"

"Yeah. Dad has been bringing me out here a long time, and it kind of runs in the family. Doesn't matter what we pick up, we're just... good."

"Good?" Harper repeats, finally meeting my gaze, and I feel even more nervous because I can't tell how she feels about all this.

"Um, good shots. Just a weird talent with us," I try to explain, running a hand through my hair. "Doesn't really matter which weapon we use, we just... always hit the target. I think it's why we have so many different types."

"That's impressive."

"Thanks." Moving closer to her, I reach for her hand and I'm relieved when she lets me take it, squeezing back. "I promise we're not crazy, doomsday preppers. Hunting is just a tradition in our family, and it works because we're good at it."

"Have you ever done any competitions?"

"Dad wouldn't let us," I answer, and she looks at me again, a furrow appearing between her brows.

"What? Why not?"

"I don't know. He's just weird about it." Shrugging, I look around the room, the smell of it bringing back so many memories. "Dad always told us that these weren't toys, that they're for hunting, not playing with. When I was a kid he got pissed when I did an archery thing in Cub Scouts. I did really well even though I'd never used a bow before, but he ended up pulling me out after that happened. That's when he started bringing me up here."

"I had no idea your dad was so intense about this stuff."

You have no idea.

"It's not a big deal, I promise. Want to see something really cool?" I ask, changing the subject as I let go of her hand to walk to the end of the room. Harper doesn't answer, but she follows me as I crouch down in front of the old chest and open it. Unwrapping the old bow from the cloth, I lift it out carefully. "This is the oldest thing in here. My dad doesn't even know who exactly owned it, but it's definitely over a hundred years old."

"Wow, it's beautiful." Leaning closer, Harper gently brushes her fingers over the delicate carvings in the wood. The little stags leap and run through intricate patterns and I'm as drawn in by them as the first time Dad showed it to me.

"Yeah. There was a commitment to craftsmanship a long time ago, you know? People put their heart and soul into these things." Adjusting my hold on the bow, I stand up and lift it like I'm going to fire, and it feels good. Right. Like it was meant for my hand. The well-worn area of the grip fits perfectly, and the wood feels surprisingly warm as I imagine an arrow in my hand, the woods all around me.

Hunt.

I can almost feel the arrow notching in place as I mime the movement, my fingers tingling as I remember the last time Dad and I hunted out here. The buck had appeared through the trees, moving carefully through the underbrush, but in the still silence I'd been able to hear every rustle of leaves. Dad had touched my elbow, signaling he wanted me to take the shot, and I'd raised my bow quietly, drawn back the string, and—

"Jared!" Harper grabs my shoulder, turning me toward her, and for a second I'm annoyed that she ruined my shot, but then I realize I'm staring at the wall of the storage room.

"What's wrong?"

"Babe, I said your name like three times. You kind of zoned out there for a minute. Are you okay?" she asks, and I can see sincere concern on her face.

"I'm fine. I was just thinking about the last time Dad and I were here," I answer, flashing a smile as I lean down to put the bow away. "Sorry I spaced out."

"No problem. That pose was kind of hot anyway." Harper's voice has that flirtatious edge that always gets me going, and I have some very good ideas for how I want to spend the evening now.

"I'm so glad you liked it," I reply, running my fingers over the carvings on the bow before I cover it again and close the chest. "Come on, let's watch a movie."

"You have a TV here?" Leading the way out of the storage room, Harper glances back over her shoulder at me. "This is definitely glamping."

"You're absolutely right," I concede with a laugh, pausing at the entrance to look back at the room, my gaze lingering on the chest before I force myself to turn off the light and shut the door. "But how else was my dad supposed to keep us entertained if it was pouring rain?"

"Ghost stories?" she suggests, and I laugh as we head back into the living room.

"I'm sure there's a few scary movies if that's what you're in the mood for."

"I'm in the mood for a lot of things," Harper replies with a wicked grin, and all I want to do is grab her and toss her on the bed — but I hold back, pushing the urge down.

"Like charades?" I joke, and she drops onto the couch and tosses one of her shoes at me from the floor. Catching it, I grin. "Okay, no charades. Yahtzee? Chutes and ladders? Checkers?"

"Would you shut up and get over here?"

"Whatever you say, babe," I reply, dropping her shoe to run and jump onto the couch, pinning her underneath me. Her laughter has me changing my mind from kissing her to tickling her just to hear more.

"Oh my God! Jared! Stop it!" Her shouts are stilted, broken up by her hysterical cackling as I find the spot on the inside of her hip that always sends her into another fit of laughter. "Stop, stop, stop!"

Planting my hand beside her waist to hold me up, I grin down at her. "This isn't what you had in mind?"

"Not at all," she says, her face still flushed as she grabs my shirt and pulls me into a kiss.

I'd planned to watch a movie with her, teasing her until she was begging for me before I took her to bed, but… we can always watch the movie after. Or tomorrow.

Since I came earlier, I know I'll have plenty of stamina to drive her crazy, to make her come over and over before we both crash.

CHAPTER FOUR
Jared

The pink tinge in the sky is beautiful, and I pause for a moment to look up at the way the clouds seem to glow with the sunrise, bouncing back vibrant oranges and pale golds amidst the pink hue. The dusky purple of night is disappearing to the west, and I take a deep breath of the cool air as I enjoy the birds and the sound of the wind moving through the trees.

I almost wish I'd given in to the urge to wake Harper up, just so she could see the land like this, but it was too early, and I'd promised she could sleep in.

And taking her hunting out here would have been too far.

That thought keeps tugging at me. Like

I'm doing something wrong by having her here, but I know Dad would understand — *will* understand.

Movement catches my eye, and I look down the ridge to see a deer moving through the trees, picking its way over the rocks sticking out of the ground around the dry creek bed. Everything gets sharper as I focus on the buck, watching carefully to make sure it's old enough. Technically, I shouldn't be hunting at all this time of year, but Dad has always said that when we're hunting on our land, to stock our fridge, the rules don't matter.

But I'm using a bow just in case.

Pulling an arrow, I notch it without having to look. This part of hunting has always felt second-nature, as easy as breathing, and I only glance down at the ground in front of me for a second as I move toward the deer.

The buck raises its head and I freeze. It's a big one with a good spread on the antlers, even though they're still coated in velvet at this time of year — but it's perfect. It will definitely fill the freezer, and I'll have more than enough to share with friends when we get home.

It leans down again and I move slowly forward. I'd ignored the doe I saw first because I knew she could still be tending to some fawns, but I hadn't worried about it. There's something about these woods, *our* woods, that mean we always find what we need. Of course, if I told Harper that she'd probably laugh it off or weave it into her conspiracy theory about our 'secret' cabin... but some things just can't be explained.

Raising the bow, I aim, pulling back the string until I can feel the strain, but then the light shifts. It's like the trees above moved in the breeze and let more light through for a moment, but it's not right. The sunrise is warm and golden, and this is... colder. Almost like fog, or mist, except I can see through it perfectly.

Well, almost perfectly.

There's a haze, a silvery wobble to the world behind it. Relaxing the bow, I squeeze my eyes closed, wiping them on my sleeve before I blink and look up again.

Still there.

What the fuck?

I've been in these woods for over ten years and I've never seen anything this weird. Maybe

I didn't get enough sleep? Blinking again, I try to ignore the shimmering haze and move closer to the deer that seems completely oblivious to the strange glow in the air — and the sudden silence. The birds aren't chirping anymore, and I can't even hear the leaves shifting under my boots.

This is fucking creepy.

Under any other circumstance, I'd be turning around and marching my ass back to the cabin… but the buck is so close. Practically posing for me at the base of the ridge, begging to be dinner, and I need to feed Harper something other than sandwiches on this trip. I told her I'd provide for her. I promised her venison, a real meal, and lunch meat and wheat bread aren't exactly a romantic dinner.

Shaking my head, I try to ignore the silvery effect in the air and draw the bow again just as the deer turns to look at me. Directly at me. It's like it can see me, as if it's not just looking in my direction but *at me*. The sound of the birds calling out to each other doesn't return, but I realize it's not silent anymore. There's something else in the air. A low hum, like the sound electricity makes when it's running through wires, and it's getting louder as the shimmering haze spreads, filling my peripheral vision.

I want to run, but my muscles won't listen.

Instead my chest grows tight, lungs refusing to expand as panic inches its way up my spine. I know I shouldn't be here. Something is very, very wrong.

Inside the hum I swear I can hear something more. Something like whispers, words just out of earshot, and I curse myself for not wearing hunter orange out here. It doesn't matter that this is private property, that there are signs posted and fencing along the property lines, some assholes might have decided to wander onto our land and if I get shot, it won't exactly make a difference that they're trespassing.

Harper.

The thought of her alone in the cabin, vulnerable, gives me the strength to move, but I don't move in the direction I tried to. Instead of backward, I'm walking forward. Toward the buck, away from the cabin, away from Harper.

"Stop it," I whisper, and it takes way more effort than it should have to get my voice to work. Not that any of this makes sense, I don't even know who or what the fuck I'm trying to talk to, but I don't care. I have to protect Harper.

The haze thickens as I move closer and closer to the buck, the hum so loud I can feel it in my teeth, and the damn buck isn't running. It's staring at me, and I can see what Harper meant about the look of their eyes.

Dark. Empty. Hollow.

There's something wrong with it. Abnormal. It's dangerous, and I can't let it stay in my forest. I have the arrow notched and the bow drawn back before I even think of doing it, but that's fine. It's still staring at me, waiting to die, and I'm happy to oblige.

It needs to die.

The air shifts, the silvery haze pulsing, and I swear I can see the buck exhaling more of the strange mist just before I let the arrow fly. I hear the impact and it bolts, finally moving the way a deer is supposed to — away from the hunter. While I move down the ridge, I watch it stumble its way up the other side, blood staining the hair around the arrow as it disappears into the trees at the top.

Shifting the bow onto my shoulder, calm slowly settles over me because I know it's only a matter of time before it drops. Adrenaline will keep it going for a bit, but I know the shot was true. They always are.

When I crest the other side of the ridge, the shimmer in the air is still present, but my eyes are glued to the blood trail on the leaves. I can't focus on the weird hum, the strange whispery sounds, or the haze. None of that matters. I have to find the buck.

I'm not sure how long I've walked when I finally see it in the shadow of a big oak tree. Everything is denser here, the sunrise not quite able to permeate the canopy above, and as I move closer, I can tell it's already gone. Chest still, mouth open, and one black, empty eye staring up at the branches.

As I pull off my backpack and prep the buck to field dress it, I can't ignore the strange sounds any longer. The hum is constant, the almost-words filtering through like someone talking in another room.

"Shut up," I growl as I pull out my knife to make the first cut, but the haze only grows thicker. Surrounding me and the buck until it could be twilight instead of dawn beneath the ancient branches of the oak.

Gritting my teeth, I plunge the blade in and my heart stops as my hand touches smooth skin instead of deer hair. Blood floods around the knife as I look up into Harper's face, but she's already gone. Empty eyed and still.

"NO!" I shout, shoving myself away from her as the hum becomes painful in my ears. Squeezing my eyes shut, I cover my ears to try and block it out. "STOP! This can't be happening. This can't be happening."

No, no, no, no, no.

I wouldn't hurt Harper. I'd never hurt Harper.

I'm pretty sure I'm going to throw up, but when I open my eyes again, she's gone. There's just the buck and my knife in the leaves beside it. Shaking my head, I try to get a deep breath, but I can't. The sound is turning into a roar, making me dizzy, and I crawl closer to the deer just to confirm that it's real. That it's not somehow Harper.

Just as I touch it, the roaring hum disappears, leaving my ears ringing for a moment in its absence. But in the silence, I can hear whispers, a woman's voice, still too quiet to make out.

And then, as if she were speaking right against my ear, I hear one thing perfectly clear. '*Loxley*!'

There's so much hate and rage in the voice that I feel it like a crushing weight. I can't breathe, can't think, there's only the silver haze coating me and the buck as the shadows grow at the edge of my vision.

"Stop," I whisper into the frigid mist, my hand landing on the knife when I reach out to steady myself.

'*Thisss isss your fate,*' the voice hisses, echoing off the trees, overlapping, and I shake my head, trying to clear my vision as the haze dims.

"No… not me." I shake my head harder, clenching the handle of the knife in my fist, prepared to fight for my life.

'*LOXLEY*!' the voice roars, and then there's only black.

My hands are cold, joints stiff, and as I force

my fingers to open around the hilt of the knife, I realize they're sticky with blood. Stumbling backward, I hit something, and a loud *clap* makes me jump and spin around.

It's a freezer.

The big freezer. In the cellar.

Shaking my head, I almost touch my forehead before I remember the blood and stop. My head is pounding, mouth dry, and an uncomfortable feeling of 'wrong' has settled deep in my bones.

What the fuck happened?

Looking at the table, I can see a mostly butchered deer, but I don't remember bringing it back. I remember seeing a doe and deciding not to shoot… and then I saw a buck and… nothing. There's a hole in my memory. An empty space. I must have shot it, but why can't I remember field dressing it? Hauling it? Butchering it?

Moving closer to the deer, I see the bags of ice piled around what's left of it. But those hadn't been down here. I'd thrown them in the freezer upstairs when we were unpacking the cooler, which means I brought them down after I killed the deer and hauled it back.

Harper.

Raw fear surges through me with adrenaline on its heels, and I don't know why I'm suddenly so panicked but I'm moving on pure instinct. Daylight pours in from the open cellar doors as I race up the stairs and run around the side of the house. When I throw open the door to the mud room, I shout for her, "HARPER!"

A second later and I'm standing in the living room, breathing hard, but I don't see her anywhere. Images of her dead and bloody flash through my head, and I'm pretty sure I'm about to be sick.

"HARPER!" I call out for her again, moving toward the bedroom when she steps out of the kitchen.

"Jared? What's wrong?" Her eyes go wide, and she turns to set her coffee down on the counter before she rushes over to me. "Oh my God, are you okay? Are you bleeding? What happened?"

My knees threaten to give out when I see her, but I just grab onto her arms instead, needing to feel her, to touch her, to hold her. "You're okay. You're okay."

"Is there a reason I wouldn't be?" she asks, and even though all I want to do is hold her, I let go when she shoves at my stomach. "You're covered in blood, Jared. What the fuck happened?"

"I..." *don't know what happened but I just snapped out of it downstairs, holding a knife, and unconsciously butchering a deer. No big deal.*

Yeah, definitely can't say that.

Holding onto her arm, I finally feel my heart slowing down again, all of the panic bleeding out of me as a strange feeling of happiness replaces it. When I try to explain, a laugh escapes instead, and it sounds a little too close to hysterical Joker level crazy for my own comfort, but Harper is okay. Harper is safe.

Even though I have no fucking idea why I thought she wouldn't be.

"I'm fine. I just..." Shrugging, I laugh again. "I just got worried about you."

"Babe, I've only been up for like an hour. I took a shower and made coffee and I'm almost done with breakfast. I was going to come out and find you when it was ready." Stepping back from me, she looks at her arms and wrinkles her nose. "Although I'm pretty sure I need another shower now. Is this deer blood?"

"Yeah, sorry. I probably should have washed up before I came inside."

"That would have been a good idea," she says, but there's still a slight frown on her face, her brows pinched together with worry. "Are you sure you're okay, babe? You sounded completely terrified."

Shaking my head, I almost shove my hand in my hair again before I stop myself and spread my arms wide instead. "Perfectly fine, and I'm almost done with the deer, so we'll have plenty to eat while we're here, and a ton to bring home."

"That's good…" Harper sounds like someone talking to a wild dog, trying not to scare it off or make it angry, but I can't really blame her when I busted in here covered in blood like a psycho.

"Tell me what you want for dinner. Venison steaks? Dad has a grinder in one of the kitchen cabinets if you want me to make that ground venison casserole we had the last time we saw them. Just tell me what you're in the mood for." Keeping the smile on my face, I dance backward to the mud room door. "Come on, babe. Who's your king of the outdoors?"

She stares at me for another second before finally rolling her eyes and turning back to the kitchen. "You decide, babe. Just clean up before you come back inside, okay?"

"Anything for you!" I call over my shoulder as I turn to the mud room, noticing the smears of blood on the door. There's more on the back door, and I shake my head as I head around the house and down into the cellar. "Great job, Jared. Freak Harper the fuck out. That's how you show her a romantic weekend. A-plus, genius fucking move."

Grumbling under my breath, I head to the freezer to see what all I accomplished in my weird blackout. There's stacks of steaks wrapped in paper and a few plastic packages of the other meat that can turn into pretty much anything else. To be honest, I'm kind of impressed at how well I did while I was apparently off in fucking lalaland.

Practice makes perfect?

If I ever had the balls to tell Dad what happened to me this morning, I'm sure he'd be proud of me, but this is an event I'm taking to the goddamn grave. It has to be some side-effect of driving all day yesterday and only getting four or five hours of sleep — even though I felt fine when I got outside this morning. And I don't feel tired now.

But Harper is perfectly safe, and that's all that matters.

A hot shower was exactly what I needed. I feel more human, more functional, now that I'm clean and dressed. Of course, I'd feel even better if I could actually remember what the fuck happened this morning… but that doesn't seem like it's going to happen.

It's like I fast-forwarded through time, skipping everything between when I saw the buck and when I snapped out of it in the cellar.

But everything is fine now.

I'm okay. Harper is okay. I have all the arrows I left with, which means I didn't try and take anything else down. The deer's carcass is taken care of, we've got good food for the special dinner I have planned tonight… and the weekend is still on track.

Digging to the bottom of my duffel bag, I feel for the edges of the box and pull it out, popping the lid. The little diamond isn't very impressive, definitely not as nice as what some of those yuppie fucks in Connecticut could buy her, but I still think she'll like it. The girl at the jewelry store had been so excited to help me, and when I'd told her how much Harper liked vintage styles, she'd hurried off to gather different options.

This engagement ring was the third one she showed me, and I'd known the second she lifted it that it was the right one. It's both simple and complex with the way the metal looks like it's woven around the tiny diamonds on either side of the round stone in the center. The total diamonds aren't even half a carat, but I still think it's pretty. The sales lady had described it as *delicate*, and although I'd never use that word to describe Harper — it still fits her. I know she deserves more, and one day I'll be able to replace it with something nicer. Something that might be worthy in the eyes of her family.

She just has to say yes first.

Tilting it toward the light, I try and imagine how she'll react when I ask her. Will she be surprised? Will she jump around like she did when she aced her Biology final? Will she do that girly scream thing that happens in the movies? I don't think she'll cry, but she might. A happy cry, of course, but normally she only gets like that when she's watching a movie about animals.

"How are you feeling, babe?" Harper calls out from the living room, but I can hear her footsteps approaching and I quickly shut the ring box and shove it back to the bottom of the bag.

"Much better," I reply, standing up just as she appears in the doorway. I'm smiling, but she's still wearing that concerned look from earlier when I scared the shit out of her. Forehead wrinkled, brows pulled together, she's got her lips pursed and her mouth tilted to the side like she doesn't believe me at all. "A shower is just what I needed. I promise, I'm all good."

"Okay. I'll heat up some food for you, then maybe we can chill for a bit. Take a nap or something."

"I don't need a nap, babe," I say, following her into the living room. "We've got to head up to Mitchell Mountain soon or we'll lose the light on the way back."

"We can do the big hike tomorrow. There's no rush." Her voice is so casual as she glances over her shoulder at me with a small smile, but I feel my stomach clench.

"I really want to take you up there today."

"Is the mountain going to disappear tomorrow?" Harper asks, and her laugh as she takes the foil off a plate feels like sandpaper on my nerves.

"No, the mountain will still be there. But… we have plenty of time to go up there today, and if we eat fast we'll be up there at the perfect time for some awesome views."

"Jared, you left before dawn to go hunting, and then you were all badass king of the outdoors turning that deer into food downstairs." Putting the plate in the microwave, she turns it on and leans against the counter to look at me. "Can't we just do a shorter hike closer to the cabin this afternoon? We can go whenever you want tomorrow."

Gritting my teeth, I try to think of some way to get her to go with me today. *This* was the plan. Ask her to marry me today, at the top of Mitchell Mountain, and then spoil her with a romantic, homecooked dinner from a deer I hunted for us. Then we'd get to spend the next two days having sex on every surface of the cabin, spending time as just us before we head home and tell everyone.

"I want us to go today, Harper. I feel fine. I don't want a nap, I don't need one, and I really want you to see it."

"Jared…" Harper sighs and crosses her arms, her gaze on the floor between us as she shakes her head and my stomach twists.

Did she find the ring while I was out? Is the trying to avoid me asking her?

"Come on, babe. I thought you loved hiking?"

"I do!" she replies, spreading her arms as she finally looks up at me again. "I love going on hikes with you, and I'm sure the views are epic, I just want to stay closer to the cabin this afternoon."

"Why!" My voice is sharper, louder than I meant for it to be.

"I'd just rather go tomorrow, okay? Please?" The microwave beeps, and she turns away to pop the door open, as if the stupid food is more important than asking her to marry me.

"Why won't you stop arguing and just go with me today?" I snap, trying to rein in my frustration, but the groan she lets out just ramps it up further.

"*Why*? Are you serious, Jared? You freaked out earlier, came in here covered in blood yelling for me, acting super weird, and you're obviously exhausted. You didn't sleep enough. Your eyes are all bloodshot, you look tired, and whether you think so or not you need a freaking nap, *not* a long hike up a mountain. We can go tomorrow!"

"Would you shut up about the goddamn nap? I'm not a fucking toddler, Harper! I don't need you telling me when it's naptime or snack time like some fucking kid!" I shout, and I'm as surprised by the outburst as she looks. Shoving a hand into my hair, I grip it at the root, pushing back the sudden anger when I see Harper's face goes blank and I know she's upset. *Stupid, stupid, stupid.* "Ughhh! Fuck, I'm sorry."

"Here's your fucking breakfast, or lunch. Whatever it is now. Eat it, or don't, it's up to you." Shoving the plate onto the counter, Harper shakes her head and sidesteps past me.

I almost reach out and grab her arm, but I stop myself, my hand hovering in the air as she moves into the living room. "Harper, wait. I'm sorry. I didn't mean it."

"What the hell was that, Jared? Since when is me trying to take care of you treating you like a toddler? That was… absolutely not okay." She crosses her arms again, her whole body tense as she stares at me, and I can tell by the way she keeps pressing her lips together that she wants to say more.

"I don't know why I said that. It was stupid." Moving forward a few steps, I stop when she shifts backward. "I'm really sorry."

"You should be. That was some major asshole shit." Shaking her head, Harper's gaze bounces around the room for a minute before she continues. "For the record, I'm not treating you like a fucking toddler. I'm *worried* about you. You look exhausted, and I know you didn't sleep much, so fuck me for suggesting we relax this afternoon! Honestly, I don't care if you take a nap or not, I just don't want you pushing yourself so hard you ruin the rest of the weekend for yourself."

"You're right, Harper. That was over the line. I was an asshole. Obviously, I'm more tired than I thought, because you know me, babe. I'm not that guy. I'm sorry I snapped at you like that, and I promise you it'll never happen again."

"Ever," she replies, her voice still carrying a hard edge that's hovering somewhere between angry and hurt — which makes sense. I've never talked to her like that, to *anyone* like that. I don't even know where that reaction came from.

"I swear." Moving to the counter, I pick up the plate and smile at the omelet she made me. It's exactly how I always make it for myself — chives, ham, and way too much cheese. Carrying it into the living room, I stop a few steps away from her. "So, I think I need a snack and a nap… and maybe a time out for being such a dick."

It takes a second, but eventually Harper's stern expression cracks and she smiles a little.

"A time out?"

"Yep. After naptime I might need a refresher course in basic social skills too."

"Social skills? Like what?"

"You know… don't chew with your mouth open, don't pee on the toilet rim, don't yell at your girlfriend when she's being awesome and made you some delicious food. The basics." I grin and she laughs quietly as she walks over to the table and sits down.

"That might be a good idea. Perhaps we could review those social skills while we take a short hike? Watch the sunset?"

"Sounds like a plan, babe. Maybe I can make a fire and we can even roast some s'mores tonight."

"I think that's a great idea." Harper's smile lights up her entire face, and I hate myself for making it disappear for even a minute.

"I love you so much, you know that?"

"I love you, too. Now, come sit with me. Please?" She pats the place beside her, and I wink at her.

"Just need to grab some water." Setting my plate on the table, I'm just glad I didn't ruin the whole fucking weekend with my bullshit outburst. "Want something to drink?"

"I'll take some water, too."

"You got it, babe." Turning back to the kitchen to get glasses for us, I try to adjust my plans for the weekend. Asking her tomorrow won't be so bad, and Harper is right anyway. I'm clearly not as up for the hike as I thought I was, and we'll still have a full day to ourselves to celebrate.

If she says yes.

The nagging thought pulls at my brain as I fill our glasses, but I refuse to give into it. I know she loves me, and I love her. We're young, but plenty of people get engaged at twenty-one, and there's no one else in the world I want to spend my life with.

I want Harper. Forever.

Waiting one more day won't matter.

CHAPTER FIVE
Harper

"No... 's not me. Not me." Jared's muttering pulls me out of sleep again, and I turn over to rub his arm, but he jerks away from me and curls up, still mumbling.

I have no idea what's going on with him, but this is the third time he's woken me up tonight talking in his sleep, and I'm pretty sure he's never done it before. I tried to wake him up the first time but he sort of... growled at me. Not a sexy, playful growl, but something bordering on threatening. It was strange, and I'd stayed awake until he calmed down again, eventually brushing it off as him having a bad dream before I fell back to sleep.

But now I'm sure something is wrong.

Leaning over the side of the bed, I tap my phone to see the time and the screen comes to life to give me bad news. It's almost four AM, and I feel like I've barely slept. Great. Our phones are useless for most things up here since there's no service, but I know it's a reliable clock.

More reliable than the ancient alarm clock on the bedside table anyway.

Sitting up, I try not to shift the mattress too much as I watch Jared twitch and grumble. He's breathing hard and I don't like the sound of it. I gently lay the back of my hand against his temple, and I'm surprised by how cool he feels to the touch. Based on how worn out he looked when we were getting ready for bed, I was sure he was getting sick.

Do people get cold before they spike a fever?

My friend Michelle is pre-med, and I'm sure she'd know the answer to that question — but I can't text her. Or call her. Hell, I can't call 911 either if he gets really sick.

Fuck, fuck, fuck.

Jared mumbles something again, but then he starts to settle down, and I carefully get out of bed. Everything creaks in this place, but I do my best to make as little noise as possible as I walk over to the closet. When I made the bed, I'd noticed another heavy blanket at the top, and maybe if I can warm him up, he'll feel better.

Every floorboard feels like it's too loud in the silence, and I'm sure the sound of the doorknob twisting is going to wake him... but when I turn around, he's still curled up on the edge of the bed. Taking a deep breath, I pull the blanket down and shake it out. I feel the dust in the air a second before I sneeze, and then sneeze again.

"What the fuck," Jared says as he sits up with a jerk and I curse myself.

"I'm sorry, babe. I just wanted to get you another blanket." Walking closer, I start to drape it over him, but he catches my arm in a hard grip.

"Why?" he asks, and I wish I could see him better in the dim light from the windows.

"You were talking in your sleep and it woke me up. When I felt your forehead, you were kind of cold, so I—"

"I don't talk in my sleep." Jared sounds gruff, irritated, but I know that neither of us have had a restful night.

"It's okay, babe. I think the extra blanket will help." I try to tug my arm free, but his fingers dig in harder. "Jared, you're hurting me. Let go."

"Okay... I see how it is," he mutters as he releases me, immediately swinging his legs out of bed to get up. "I'm *hurting* you. I'm waking *you* up. Well, I guess I'm nothing but trouble to you."

"I didn't say that!" I argue, but he's already stomping toward the doorway. "Jared! Where are you going?"

"I'm going to sleep on the couch. Wouldn't want to disturb your sleep anymore."

"Jared, stop it. Just come back to bed," I plead, but he walks into the living room like he didn't even hear me. Following, I find him crouched in front of the fireplace, stoking it back to life as he adds a few more logs. "What are you doing?"

"It's fucking cold in here, so I'm getting the fire going. Is that okay with you?" he snaps, and I'm speechless for a moment. Something is definitely wrong with him, but I don't know how to fix it.

"Babe, did you have a nightmare?"

"What?" He jabs the poker into the smoldering coals over and over, his bare shoulders catching the dull, red light as his muscles shift under his skin.

"I... I was just wondering if you had bad dreams. You were telling someone 'no' in your sleep, and—"

"You already told me I was waking you up, it's why I'm out here. Just go back to bed, Harper." There's none of his normal sweetness in his voice, and I want to remind him that I never said I wanted him to sleep on the couch, but I have a feeling it will only cause more issues. We're both exhausted and talking about it in the early hours of the morning isn't going to help things.

Without replying to him, I head back into the bedroom and grab the blanket I'd pulled down for him. When I come back out to the living room, he's sitting cross-legged in front of the fireplace, watching the renewed flames as they start licking at the fresh wood. "Do you want me to stay out here with you?"

"Not enough room," he mumbles, and I lay the blanket over the arm of the couch as I waver between staying up with him or going back to bed.

"Well… I don't think we had that problem before. I remember us making the most of the space on the couch." I give him a smile when he turns around to look at me, but it slowly fades when he doesn't return it.

"It's late. Just go get some sleep, Harper."

"Okay. I love you," I say, moving toward the doorway slowly as I watch him focus on the fire again.

"Love you too," he eventually replies, but there's none of the normal emotion in his voice when he says it back, and I try not to let it bother me as I leave the bedroom door open and climb into bed. It's noticeably colder without him in it, and I burrow under the blanket, angling myself so I can watch the steadily growing glow from the living room.

I can't fall asleep right away because I can't stop worrying about him. Jared isn't acting like himself, and all I want is to figure out what's wrong so I can help. He's the only guy I've ever felt so strongly about, and I never would have moved in with him if I didn't think we had a future together… but is this some snapshot of what a life with him could be like?

The thoughts keep spinning in my head. A hundred different issues that could be going on with him from being sick to being sick of *me*. I don't want to believe that, and all of my instincts tell me that he loves me, but there's some kind of wall between us right now that I can't breach.

He's just tired, and so are you.

Sighing, I roll onto my back and watch the light dance over the painting above the bed. It's on wood instead of canvas, and when I asked about it, Jared just said it was their 'family crest.' The green and burgundy tones are hard to see in the dim light, but the gold paint catches the light, making the crossed arrows and the flower stand out in the darkness. I have no idea if my family even has a crest, or what it would look like, but his is beautiful. Mesmerizing. The flickering firelight in the living room almost makes it look like they're moving, dancing, drawing attention to the bold lines of his family name written beneath the crest.

LOXLEY.

It's a name I've imagined paired with my own just as often as I've imagined a future with the man who carries it. *Jared and Harper Loxley.* It just flows, like it was meant to be.

Like we were meant to be.

When I wake up again, the bedroom is bright and sunny, and the cabin definitely feels warmer. Rolling to the side of the bed, I tap my phone to check the time and I'm out of bed the second the numbers register in my brain.

Ten-thirty? Why didn't Jared wake me up?

Moving into the living room, I see the couch is empty, but the fire is still going strong, which means he can't be far.

"Jared?" I call out but standing in the living room there aren't many places in the cabin he could be where I wouldn't see him. Still, when I don't hear a reply I peek into the kitchen, the bathroom, and the other bedroom before I head into the mud room. I cleaned up the smears of blood he'd left behind yesterday, but I double-check the doors as I rap my knuckles against the door to the weird room of weapons. "Babe?"

There's no answer again, but in the silence I catch a dull *thump* from outside. When I open the back door, I don't see him, but a few seconds later I hear a louder *thwack* and I'm sure he has to be out here somewhere. Hurrying back into the bedroom, I toss on clothes and shoes, more aware of the occasional *thumps* coming from outside. They're not exactly consistent, but they keep coming even as I walk out the backdoor and into the cool breeze. Following the sound around the side of the house, I find Jared chopping wood. His shirt is stuck to his skin with sweat, and there's already a solid pile of split logs beside him.

"Making more firewood for us, babe?" I ask, smiling at him as I walk closer, but he barely spares me a glance before he brings the axe down, splitting the log in front of him in half. He grabs the piece that stayed atop the old tree stump, rotates it, and then brings the axe down again to split it. "Jared?"

"The cabin is too cold. You need firewood to be comfortable and we're running low." His deadpan reply doesn't sound like him at all, but at least he's being nicer in the daylight.

"I'm sure we have enough for a few days, babe, and it's not that cold inside."

"We need more," he says as he picks up the other half of the original log and puts it in place. The axe lands with a heavy *thwack*, the strained sound of the wood splitting feels a bit like nails on a chalkboard to me and I flinch.

"How long have you been up, babe?"

Jared doesn't respond, he doesn't even look at me. He just sets the axe down, walks over to pick up another log, and brings it back to the chopping block. I'm not sure if it's a trick of the mountain light, but he looks oddly pale even though he's dripping sweat.

Maybe he is sick.

"Did you make something to eat already?" I move closer to him, and he finally looks at me for real. There's a lost look to him, something about the way his eyes never stop moving over my face, and all I want is for him to come inside and sit down. "I can make us something to eat."

"I'm not hungry," he answers, picking the axe up before he lands it again. My king of the outdoors providing again, even though it's not necessary. One glance at the wood pile against the cabin, half-hidden under a tarp, shows that we have more than enough wood even if we wanted to keep the fire going all day and night until we left.

"I can make a venison scramble?" I'm trying to tempt him by using the deer he took down yesterday, and for a second I think it's working because he looks at me, but then he's back to chopping wood.

"Make whatever you want." The words are spoken quickly, in between two huffs of effort to crack the log into firewood, but there's no interest.

"When did you want to go to the mountain?" I ask, hoping that will snap him out of it, but he just brings the axe down hard, sending a piece of wood flying as he starts to laugh. Low and soft.

"Oh, so *now* you want to go see the mountain? I thought you wanted to 'chill,' Harper. Relax, stick close to the cabin, etcetera, etcetera." Jared shakes his head, yanking the axe free of the stump, but instead of grabbing another piece of wood he raises his arm and points the axe at me. "Why don't you go do that? Go on. Go *chill*. Relax. Let me handle everything else."

"What are you talking about, Jared? We said we were going on the hike today. I just wanted you to rest yesterday because you weren't feeling well."

"Yeah, and we talked about leaving this morning, but that obviously wasn't important to you." His words feel like a slap, and for a moment all I can do is stare at him, but I recover quickly.

"If you wanted to leave earlier, why didn't you wake me up? Why are you out here chopping firewood when we clearly have plenty?" Throwing my arm out toward the pile of firewood, he barely glances at it before he turns his gaze back to the chopping block so he can add another piece of wood.

"If you don't want me, Harper. All you have to do is say it. You don't have to—"

"Are you fucking kidding me?" I shout, and that seems to get his attention. "Of course, I want you! I fucking love you. I love you even though you've been so weird about this trip, and increasingly weird since we got here. I'm just trying to make you some fucking food so we can go on this hike to the mountain!"

"If you wanted to go, you would have been up earlier." He turns away, mumbling something else under his breath, and I can feel my temper flaring as he walks over to a mossy pile of logs and drags another back to the block.

"I was up all night worrying about *you*, jackass! You were talking in your sleep, telling someone 'no' over and over, and a bunch of other shit. If you wanted to leave earlier, all you had to do was wake me up!"

Jared doesn't even look at me, much less respond, and I storm over to him, grabbing onto the arm he has the axe in, which finally makes him see me... but up close he looks even worse. His eyes are majorly bloodshot, and I'd swear he's lost weight overnight with the way his skin looks pulled tight against his cheekbones and jaw.

"Babe, I'm worried about you," I whisper, softening my voice, and for a second he looks like him again. His green eyes come to life, his smile twitches the edge of his mouth upward, and I lean into his hand when he brings it up to my cheek.

"I'm fine, Harper. I promise. If you're hungry, you should eat. I just need to get some stuff done around here."

"Do you still want to go to the mountain today?" I ask, and he leans in to kiss me. It's almost chaste compared to how he usually kisses me, but at least it's *something*.

"Maybe later, maybe tomorrow. We'll see." His answer isn't an answer at all, but he releases me and tilts his chin toward the cabin. "Go on and make us something to eat. I'll be in later."

I grab his hand, forcing his fingers to interlace with mine so I can squeeze hard. "I love you, Jared."

"And I love you, Harper. More than you can possibly understand," he whispers, leaning his forehead down to mine as he squeezes my hand back, and for some reason I feel like crying. His tone almost sounds pleading when he speaks again. "Please go back inside."

"Okay." I nod, stepping back to release him, and I'm relieved to see *my* Jared. The man who makes me laugh and smile and feel so incredibly loved every single day. "I'll come check on you after I make something to eat, okay?"

"No need, babe." Lifting the axe again, he gestures toward the cabin. "Go on inside, I'll be in when I'm done out here."

"Don't be long, okay?" I try another smile, but I don't think he sees it as he positions another log on the block. When I turn around to go inside, I hear the heavy *thwack* of the axe, and I'm not sure if this is an improvement over yesterday or not.

I didn't make breakfast, or lunch, which feels kind of petty, but I'm definitely feeling petty right now. Jared made such a big deal about this weekend, about how we were going to have so much fun, how we were going to go somewhere really *special*, and every minute has been more miserable than the last. I can still hear the random swings of the axe, which means he's still avoiding me by cutting up firewood that neither of us need — but I tried. I tried to get him to come inside, I tried to be a good girlfriend, and whatever weird shit is going on in his head right now... he's obviously not interested in letting me in.

Shoving the spoon back into my yogurt, I continue wandering the cabin, but Jared had been right that there wasn't much to it. The only rooms with anything interesting are the living room with its random collection of DVDs, and the large bedroom where a narrow, built-in bookshelf is stocked with books on animals and plants and others with no titles at all. Grabbing one of the canvas-backed ones with no title, I drop onto the bed and open it to a random page.

The handwriting throws me at first, but I quickly realize it's not a fancy book... it's a journal. His dad's journal, if I'm understanding the notes correctly.

November 3, 2013 — Took Jared and Oliver hunting SE toward creek. Found nesting area near tall oak and bird beak rock outcropping. Got a buck near the old beaver dam.

I can't find a signature or anything, but based on what Jared has told me, his grandfather never brought them out here. Just his dad.

Flipping through the pages, I find a ton of little descriptions where Jared's dad was teaching them about tracking, about the woods and the land, or making notes on where they hunted, but I stop on a page where I see a note unrelated to hunting or deer or the landscape. It's tucked under a note from 2015 where both Jared and his brother had been out with their dad, but his father only mentions one of them.

I need to talk to Jared about the rules of the land. Have to do it before he comes out on his own.

He was sixteen when his father made that note, and while I'm curious about the first time his dad let him come out here on his own to hunt… I'm way more interested in the reference to the 'rules.' I quickly flip through the last of the book, and then I set it aside and look for older journals. Grabbing a worn, leather-bound copy, I open it to the middle and find a reference to the year 1992.

January 9, 1992 — Charlie and I walked the northern border today, found two nests from overnight near the grove of ash with the open meadow and the circle stone. We will focus on a buck in the morning.

Charles Loxley is Jared's dad, and it feels a little eerie to be reading about the man as a kid.

I'm not even sure how old he was in 1992, but I know it was before Jared or I were born. Flipping through the journal more carefully, I skim the slanted cursive, trying to find anything that doesn't reference hunting or the property itself. I end up pulling the next leather-bound volume out of the library just to continue skimming, and when I hit 1994 I finally find something that eerily echoes the note Jared's dad made.

Charlie has a girl in his life, and I explained the Loxley rules to him. He understands the consequences now.

Leaning back against the bookshelf, I feel overwhelmed by the sheer number of volumes on the shelves. There are more without titles than I originally noticed, and the ones on the very bottom look almost too old to handle. The last thing I'd want to do is damage Jared's family's property, but the strange vaguebooking isn't helping. Sighing, I skim through the end of that journal without finding another reference to any kind of rules or 'consequences' and so I pick another. I'm only a little way into the next journal when the light shifts and I look up to find Jared in the doorway.

"What are you doing, Harper?"

CHAPTER SIX
Harper

PANIC GRABS HOLD OF MY LUNGS AND REFUSES to let go, which leaves me without much to say in response as Jared slowly walks closer.

"Get up."

"I was just looking at the books, trying to find something to read, but these are journals. Did you know these are journals?" I'm rambling now, holding out the leather-bound book as some kind of explanation, but when Jared gets to me, he just smacks it out of my hand.

"Did I say you could look through my family's things?" He asks the question so softly, but there's anger underneath the words and for the first time in my life I'm actually a little scared of him.

"I'm sorry, Jared. I didn't know I wasn't supposed to touch them, you didn't say anything about— OW!" I flinch when he suddenly grabs my hair, craning my head back as pinpricks of pain skitter across my scalp. "You're hurting me."

"Am I?" He tilts his head, his face filling my vision as he leans close, but he still doesn't let me go.

"You're scaring me, Jared," I whisper, staring into his green eyes that seem too... flat. Too empty.

"Which is it, Harper? Am I hurting you? Scaring you? Keeping you up at night? What complaint do you have about me now?" Jared lets go of my hair, but he quickly captures my face. Hands firmly planted on either side of my head so I still can't move away, trapped on my knees with his face inches from mine.

"Please stop." The words are barely audible because I'm pretty sure I'm about to cry, but then he kisses me. It's powerful, commanding, and my head swims when he yanks me off the floor by my arm and drags me toward the bed.

"You want me to stop? Stop what? Loving

you?" Jared lets out a rough laugh that sounds nothing like him as he slowly shakes his head. "I don't think I can do that, Harper."

"No! I love you, Jared, I do. I'm just worried about you!"

"You love me?" he asks, head canted to the side.

"Of course I do."

"Say it again," he commands, voice low, and I nod as he strokes his thumb over my cheek.

"I love you, Jared. I love you so much, I just—" My words are cut off when he shoves me back onto the bed, his hands on the button of my jeans before I even realize what's happening. Grabbing his hands, I try to stop him, but he gets my zipper down anyway. "Jared, stop! Would you just talk to me?"

"You keep trying to push me away," he mumbles, knocking my hands away so he can rip my jeans down, catching my underwear on the next tug. I try to twist away from him, and I manage to land a kick on his hip, but he growls at me like he did in his sleep — and it doesn't matter anyway. He tosses my clothes away and grabs my legs to drag me back toward him across the bed.

"JARED!" I scream his name, trying to snap him out of whatever the fuck this is, but then he's on top of me, kissing me, muffling my words with his lips as he spreads my legs with his. When I turn my head, breaking the kiss, he just trails them down my neck, finding that place near my collarbone that sends a thrill rushing through my blood even though all I want is for him to be normal again. To be *him* again. "Please, Jared, just listen to me."

"You say you love me, but I'm never good enough for you. That's the real problem, isn't it?" he whispers against my skin, grinding between my thighs, and I can feel his erection through the rough fabric of his jeans as I shake my head. "Is that what you were looking for in the journals? A reason to leave me?"

"No! I don't want to—" I'm cut off by Jared's hand covering my mouth, and all I can do is whine as his fingers dig into my cheek.

"No more lying." Jared shakes his head, his eyes wild as he stares down at me. "I can't let you leave me, Harper. I won't. You're mine."

I need him to listen to me, to really listen

so that he'll stop acting like this, but it's useless when I try to pull his hand away from my face. He's bigger than me, stronger, and I can feel his sweat soaking through my shirt as he presses me into the bed so he can work at his jeans.

"Show me. Show me you love me, Harper," he whispers, and all I can do is shout against his palm as I shove at his ribs, trying to get him off me, but too quickly he shifts and I feel his other hand between my legs. He pushes two fingers inside, and I whimper because I'm not wet enough for this. "I thought you loved me," he growls. "Did you lie? Do you always lie?"

NO! I try to scream it, but it just comes out as a broken vowel sound beneath the muffling effect of his hand, and then I feel his thumb on my clit. I try to shake my head, but he just holds me still, forcing me to take the dull thrums of pleasure each swirl of his thumb brings.

"Come on, I know you like this. You always want me inside you, and I'm not going to make you wait this time. I'm going to make sure you remember you're mine." There's something off in his voice, and when he takes his fingers away, I feel his cock press against me.

His bare cock. *Oh God. He doesn't have a fucking condom on!*

I try harder to knock him off, twisting my hips to keep him from thrusting inside me, but he braces his arm across my chest and pins me down just before he pushes in. I'm not ready, and the twinge of pain between my thighs freezes me in place as he groans.

"Yessss... take it." Jared rocks his hips, forcing himself deeper, and tears burn the edges of my eyes as I dig my nails into his sides. With his forearm across my chest, so close to my throat, I can't do anything. I can't even beg him to slow down, to wait for my body to adjust. He knows how thick he is and how much it can hurt, and he's always been so fucking careful with me — but he's not *my* Jared right now.

There's something wrong with him. Something very wrong. His knees push against my legs, spreading me wider, and when I cry out on the next hard thrust, he shushes me.

"I'm almost in. Almost. You can take it." He grunts and pain ricochets through me as his skin finally meets mine. All I can do is whine as he lets out a long, low moan and slides back to thrust again. "Fuck, you feel so good."

It doesn't feel good! I want to scream at him, to make him realize what he's doing because this hurts more than it usually does. He always stretches me, but he makes sure I'm wet first. Soaking and needy and *ready*, but I wasn't ready for this. Definitely not ready for him to pick up the pace already, driving in harder, our bodies clapping together with each powerful slam of his hips.

"Mine. All mine," he whispers against my ear, and I whimper because there's still an ache between my thighs… but my body is responding. I'm getting wet, adjusting to his size, and even though I still want to slap him for this, I can feel pleasure weaving its way into the complicated whirl of emotions in my head. I'm angry, hurt, worried about him, worried about *me*, but he knows just how to move to hit that place inside me that sends a buzz rushing under my skin.

When he finally takes his hand off my mouth, I pull in a gasp of air, filling my lungs for the first time in what feels like hours, but before I can shout at him, he kisses me. It's aggressive, a dominating claim of my mouth, and I lose myself in the nipping bites and sweeps of his tongue. A moment later he shifts his arm off my chest, and even though I know I should stop this — I can't.

With him kissing me, this almost feels normal. More raw, more primal than any other time we've ever been in bed together, but I can't deny the blur of pleasure humming in my blood now. I'm inching toward an orgasm, stoked by each rough drive of his hips, each seductive nip of his teeth on my skin. When he moves my hands beside me and interlaces our fingers, pinning them down, I don't even fight him. I just rock my hips to meet the next hard thrust, the dull ache blending seamlessly with the incredible friction of him moving inside me.

"Harper…" he whispers as he kisses down my neck, seeking that spot that has me moaning and urging him on with another flick of my hips.

He's never been this rough, this controlling in bed, but I've also never been this close to an orgasm this fast. Not without him teasing me, licking me until I feel like I'm going to explode. It's some strange, primal response, something

I can't control or logic myself through while he's fucking me like this. Hard, dominating. Possessive.

"Mine," he groans, biting down on my shoulder as he starts to thrust faster, letting go of one of my hands to grab my leg, bending my knee toward my chest so he can go deeper on the next drive of his hips. The low growl in his chest vibrates through my own, and I know he's close, but I'm not far behind and—

FUCK.

"Jared! Jared, stop!" I try to pull my hand free, but he tightens his grip on it and on my leg, pressing me harder into the bed as he nips at my shoulder again. Panicking, I force my free hand between us and grab his face, my hand under his jaw as I lift him enough to look into his eyes. "Condom. We need a condom, Jared. Please."

His pupils are so dilated there's just a thin ring of green around them, and at first I don't see any recognition in them, but he only thrusts once more and stops, breathing hard.

"Get a condom. Please."

"You're mine," he answers softly, voice gruff, and I nod.

"Yes, babe. I'm yours, but we need a condom, okay? Please?" Easing my hold on his face, I nod some more, and he stares at me for a long moment before he finally nods back.

"Okay." Jared looks up, eyes searching the room, and then his gaze lands back on me. "Don't move."

"I won't." I stay still as he slowly lets go of my hand and my leg, moving to brace himself on either side of my ribs. He's not looking at me though, he's staring down at where we're joined, skin to skin. We've only had sex without a condom once before, and it was because we were drunk and stupid, and I ended up taking the morning after pill the next day. He'd promised that it would never happen again, but when he's still buried inside me a few seconds later, I'm not sure if he plans on keeping that promise. "Jared?"

"I need you," he says, his voice low and rough and bordering on confused as he looks back into my eyes, his brows pulled together.

"I won't move. I promise. I want you too." Reaching up, I brush my hand across his cheek and his eyes close as he leans into my touch.

"Just get a condom and we can keep going. I'm all yours."

He nods before he opens his eyes, his intense gaze boring into me as he says, "Mine."

Finally, he slides out of me, and I'm distracted by the sight of him. He looks even bigger than usual, thick and shiny with my wetness as his cock bobs at his hips. Sitting up straight he tears his sweat-soaked shirt over his head and tosses it to the floor before he stands and lets his jeans and boxers fall as well. I don't move at all as he walks around the bed, grabbing a whole strip of condoms from the box before he returns to my side.

"Planning on another round or four?" I ask, trying to lighten the intense mood, but Jared just looks at me, his brows pulling together again as another strange expression passes over his face. After another second he tears a foil packet free and rips it open, and I finally relax a bit as he rolls it on.

"All mine," he mumbles as he climbs back onto the bed between my thighs, pushing my knees wide enough to make my hips ache. I hiss air through my teeth, but I don't fight him as he runs his thumb through my wetness, dipping it inside. I'm sore already, tender, and when he switches to his fingers my hips jerk. Two fingers quickly becomes three, and I whine from the low pulse of pain, but it fades fast when he finds my g-spot and starts to tap. Jared's voice sounds oddly flat when he quietly says, "I want you to like this."

"I do. I'm just sore," I try to explain, but it makes him frown and he shifts off the edge of the bed, immediately leaning forward to flick his tongue over my clit. A breath later he captures it and sucks, focusing on the bundle of nerves as he works his fingers inside me, sending me higher and higher until I'm fisting the sheets and arching my back from the constant waves of overwhelming sensation. "Fuck, fuck, fuck! Yes, Jared, yes…"

"Better?" he asks in that same weird tone, and when I look down at him between my thighs, I can almost see *my* Jared in the darkness of his eyes. I nod and he dips his head back down, drawing another loud moan out of me as I fight the urge to come, but it's hard when he's attacking my g-spot and my clit with such dangerous accuracy.

"Please, please," I beg, and he stops and looks up at me. I can't think of what to say, but when I reach my hand down for him, he quickly climbs back on the bed, shifting me further up until he's on the bed too.

"I…" Jared trails off, his gaze moving down my body as he slides a hand up my side, pushing my shirt higher. "I need you to be mine."

"I am yours," I answer, wiggling to pull my shirt over my head before I twist my arm underneath to unhook my bra and drop it to the floor. He groans, lowering his head to pull a nipple into his mouth, grazing the sensitive bud with his teeth before he sucks and teases, making me squirm beneath him. "Jared, please."

When he lifts his head again, I'm not sure what the look on his face means, but it's something entirely new. Everything about him feels different, but I'm not scared anymore. His tongue traces across his bottom lip before he lowers his hips between mine and grinds against me, teasing me with his hard shaft. "I need to take you. Make you mine," he whispers.

"Take me then."

His gaze seeks mine and I'm not sure where the concern is coming from until he growls and shakes his head, one hand coming up to rip at his hair. "Don't want to hurt you. Not you."

Catching his face in my hands, I rub my thumbs across his cheeks. "I'm okay."

"Promise."

"I promise." Reaching down, I wrap my fingers around his dick and squeeze as I stroke him once from tip to base, pulling him down over me with a hand on the back of his neck. "I'm okay."

That's all it takes for him to kiss me again, pressing me into the bed as his hips move between my thighs and he thrusts deep, catching my gasp with another kiss. I'm going to be sore as hell tomorrow, but it'll all be worth it if this helps him, if it makes him normal again.

"Fuck!" I bite down on a whine as he grabs a fistful of my hair again, craning my neck back so he can kiss and nip as he does exactly what he said — he takes me. This isn't making love, or even some drunken fuck after a party. It feels like ownership, like he wants to claim every inch of my skin inside and out and mark me as his.

"You have to be mine, Harper. You can't leave. Can't leave." The words come out between huffs of breath, peppered with grunts and groans as he forces one of my knees up so he can drive in deeper. Even with the dull ache that spikes each time he bottoms out, the pleasure is returning fast, spiraling up my spine like strands of shimmering, electric light. I don't know why he suddenly thinks I'd want to leave him. I don't know why he keeps picking fights with me. All I know is that I love him.

His teeth sink into that tender spot on my shoulder and I cry out, nails digging into his back as pain radiates out from it, mixed with a tease of ecstasy that shouldn't be there.

I know it shouldn't be there, that I shouldn't like it when he makes it hurt, but it's not like there hasn't always been a little pain during sex with him. Jared just never seemed to *want* to inflict it before today. He growls again, slamming deep, and he bites down harder.

"Jared! That hurts!" I whimper when he lets go, his lips crushing mine as he starts to thrust again. Brutal, hard, but the friction and the feeling of being absolutely filled is undeniable and as the pain abates there's only pleasure left behind. Overwhelming, suffocating, and all I can do is hold on as he takes me higher and higher with each powerful drive between my thighs.

"Have to make you mine," he growls, grabbing my hands to pin them above my head, but I'm so close to coming that I don't even care that my wrists hurt from how hard he's holding them down. All I can do is nod and ride the waves as they continue to build, carrying me closer to the perfect, blinding brilliance that each powerful thrust of his cock is driving me toward.

I pull against his hold on my wrists as my back arches, every muscle in my body going tight a second before the tension snaps and glittering light explodes behind my eyes. It's pure ecstasy, absolute bliss, and I can barely breathe as I cry out his name and something else that's utterly unintelligible. There's only raw pleasure pulsing through my veins, dragged out into an almost painful perfection because he's still fucking me. Just as hard, his strength rocking me against the bed as he groans in my ear.

When I finally start to come down from the orgasm, I realize he isn't as close to coming as I thought he was. Jared has barely slowed down, fucking me straight through one and already building me toward a second. I can barely breathe, moans and cries escaping with every exhale, and I think I'm pleading with him to come, but I'm not completely sure the words are actually leaving my lips. Even though my muscles are still trembling from the first orgasm, I can feel another one rising. Catastrophic, overpowering, and unlike anything else I've ever felt. This isn't what the multiples feel like when he licks me until I'm begging and then fucks me until I come again for him... this is more.

Dizzying. Devastating. Dangerous.

"Jared," I whine, gasping when he seems to swell inside me, somehow stretching me more, and then I feel it. That terrifying edge approaching too fast to avoid.

"You're mine," he growls, breathing roughly as he thrusts hard enough to bruise my hips and all the aches and torrential pleasure spiral until I cry out and the world blinks out of existence.

For a moment there's nothing but bliss, a blank void of raw sensation filled with shimmering silver light, and then it feels like something yanks me back into my body. All of the physical crashes in so fast that I can barely gasp before another orgasm breaks over me, drowning me in ecstasy again, and Jared finally shouts. Thrusting deep, his cock jerks inside me, and I can only focus enough to recognize the low groan of pleasure buzzing against my ear as he comes.

Everything is still humming though, even after he stops moving. All of my nerves are buzzing and vibrating. I can almost hear the hum of them in my ears, feel the buzzy sensation in my teeth, my skin tingling like an electric current is only inches away. My muscles keep trembling, shivers rolling through me with little aftershocks, and the weight of him on me seems to be the only thing keeping me grounded. He still smells like Jared, still feels like Jared, and even if something is wrong, I know we'll get through it together.

We'll figure it out.

Pulling in a shaky breath, I say the only thing I can think of in the chaos of my mind. "I love you."

CHAPTER SEVEN
Jared

My heart is still racing, the mind-blowing blankness of the orgasm finally fading out along with the powerful jolt of pleasure that came with it. We're both breathing hard, and she's still squeezing my cock in teasing waves as she squirms under me. Those sweet little sounds escaping her lips with every shift of her body.

But I can't move.

I'm not sure I actually want to.

If I move, if I even lift my head, I'll have to face Harper… and I don't think I can do that right now. I hurt her. I didn't want to hurt her, but I did. I know I did. Everything seems like such a blur, fuzzy, but I can remember the panic on her face when I came in the room — and then there was so much anger. A raw rage that filled my already muddled brain with darkness.

I don't know where it came from. I don't know why it was directed at her; I just know that the moment I saw her looking through the old hunting journals something inside me just snapped. I tried to rein it in, tried to rein *myself* in, because there's no one else to blame but me.

This was all me.

No one else touched her. No one else made her panic, pushed her onto the bed and ripped her clothes off. Hell... I fucked her practically dry. I *hurt* her, and I don't understand why it seemed necessary at the time. I don't know why I felt so completely sure she was going to leave me if I didn't do something about it. If I didn't make her mine somehow.

That is the one thought that's so clear in all the madness. The absolute need to claim her, to make her mine before it was too late. It pushed every other instinct away, every instinct to protect her, to take care of her, to keep her safe — all of those disappeared until all that was left was this insane need to fuck her until she gave in and submitted.

Worst of all… I don't think the feeling is gone.

Whatever is wrong with me, it's just temporarily sated. Post-nut clarity or whatever the fuck this fleeting grasp at sanity is, and if I really want to keep her safe, I should just leave. Walk away.

Fuck.

I can't. Even thinking about it makes me sick, makes me want to grab her so she can't leave me, and I don't want to hurt her. I love Harper. I love her more than anything. I want to fucking marry her, but I can't make these dark thoughts stop flickering through my brain.

Her wrists twist under my hands and I realize I'm still pinning her to the goddamn bed like a monster. It takes real effort to make my fingers unwrap from her skin, but she doesn't say anything about it. No, Harper uses her new freedom to run her hands down my back, her fingertips tracing little patterns on their way up and down.

I don't deserve her affection.

She needs to leave.

But I'm afraid of what I might do if she tried to go right now, even if I was the one who told her to do it.

My dick finally softens enough to slip out of her, and I know I need to get away from her. She probably doesn't want me on top of her anymore anyway, and that thought makes the darkness in my head ripple… which just proves how right I am. Clenching my eyes tight, I push myself up and off of her, immediately shifting up the bed until my back hits the headboard.

"Babe?" Her voice sounds too fucking sweet. She should be screaming at me, hitting me, *something*.

Pulling my knees toward my chest, I brace my elbows on them so I can cover my face with my hands. I don't want to look at her. I don't want to see whatever is waiting for me.

"Jared? Are you okay?" she asks, and I can feel the bed shifting as she moves closer to me, even though she should be doing the exact opposite. She should be running… but I can't make myself say it. "Babe?"

"I'm okay," I whisper, my voice rough like I spent all night screaming at a concert, but I don't remember screaming. I don't remember much from last night at all. Just the cold. I couldn't get warm, and even now I can feel how cool my fingers are against my face. My comfort doesn't mean anything though. I just don't know if I have the balls to ask Harper if she's okay... I don't know what I'll do if she answers the wrong way.

Hell, I don't even know what the 'wrong way' would be, but I don't trust myself at all. Not right now.

"Jared?" she says my name again and I groan, grabbing fistfuls of my hair and pulling... just like I did to her.

Be a fucking man.

"Are... are you okay?" I ask, but I keep my eyes closed tight until I hear her quiet chuckle. When I peek at her between my arms, I find her smiling a little, her brown hair mussed, lips red, and a series of bite marks across her shoulders... one of which is darker than the others and it still shows my teeth. "I'm so sorry."

"Babe, I'm fine." Harper reaches over and squeezes my arm. "I mean... that was seriously intense, and I'm not sure if I can handle the rough sex thing all the time, but"—she shrugs a shoulder, dropping her hands into her lap— "it was kind of fun."

"What?" I can't really process what she's saying, but I don't know how much of my memory I can even trust. I can see the bitemarks, so I know those were real, and her wrists are still red from where I had them pinned... but maybe I didn't hurt her? Not as bad as I think I did?

"I know you've been off the last couple of days, babe, but if this is something you want to try all you have to do is talk to me about it. You know I'm open to trying stuff, and even though I didn't like you covering my mouth, having you go all dominant alpha male every once in a while wouldn't be a bad thing." Harper laughs a bit, a blush staining her cheeks when she finally lifts her gaze from the bed to meet mine. "I definitely came a few times, so I'm happy to try it. As long as you wear a condom next time. From the beginning, okay?"

"Okay." I nod, the visual of my hand over her mouth flashing inside my head. I'd wanted to make her stop saying something. *No more lying.* That was it. But why did I think she was lying? What did I think she was lying about? Groaning, I rub at my forehead, trying to make my brain sort out the memories into something that makes sense. Anything that would make sense of this shit, but I have a sinking feeling there's something much worse underneath my confusion.

"Jared, can you talk to me? Please?" Harper moves closer, her hand brushing mine, and I immediately turn away and climb out of the bed. The hurt look on her face feels like a physical blow, but things are getting less clear by the minute.

"I— I need to use the bathroom. And, um, take care of the condom." I'm stumbling over my words as I back toward the doorway, and I'm not sure how to interpret the way Harper is staring at me, but I know I need to get away from her.

Turning around, I rush into the living room, pulling off the condom to drop in the kitchen trash before I head to the bathroom and shut the door. Leaning against it, I almost feel like I can breathe right again. My heart is still pounding, but I can't smell her or see her or grab her.

Running my hands over my face, I take a deep breath and groan.

Scratch that, I can definitely still smell her... but at least I can't see her. Can't touch her in here.

Lifting the seat on the toilet, I brace one hand on the wall and try not to fuck up and piss all over as I try to come up with a solution. Everything seemed clearer right after I came, but I can tell I'm losing that. As messed up as my head is right now, it feels like it should be the middle of the night, but the sun is still streaming through the window beside me. Mocking me with how bright and clear it is outside when I feel anything but.

I jab the handle on the toilet and turn toward the sink to wash my hands, but my reflection catches my attention and I can't look away. My eyes are so red, completely bloodshot, and there's bags under them like I pulled an all-nighter even though I know I slept last night.

A headache picks up behind my left eye and I rub at it, leaning on the sink as I groan. I remember Harper telling me I kept waking her up in the night, and I'd moved to the couch just so she could sleep.

No. That's not how it happened.

We argued, and she looked upset when I told her to go back to bed, but I don't even remember if I actually went back to sleep after that. I just remember the fire and trying to get warm... and then I started chopping firewood.

Fuck me.

Something isn't right, but I know one thing for sure. I can't lose Harper. I have to make her mine or I could lose her forever.

Wait... no. I have to keep her safe. Even if that means keeping her safe from me.

That is the most important thing right now, no matter how much it feels like I'm going to lose her. I have to ignore that. I have to fight that feeling so I don't do something terrible.

Another piercing headache lances through my head, so blinding that I feel my knees give out, and when I force my eyes open again, I'm sitting on the floor, back against the door to the narrow shower stall. The pain isn't fading though. It pulses behind my left eye like someone's jabbed a knife into it and is wiggling it around for fun. There's a low hum in my ears, almost like the sound of electricity, and it's only getting louder. A wave of nausea joins in the fun and I feel a cold sweat break out across my skin as I crawl toward the toilet, slamming the seat back down so I have something to rest against as my stomach churns.

"Jared? Are you okay?" Harper asks from the other side of the door, and I feel a wave of panic and a sudden urge to shout at her simultaneously. Clenching my teeth, I don't say anything. I can barely see straight. The sunlight is too bright, making everything glow, and I have to close my eyes against it. "Babe, I'm going to come in."

The doorknob rattles and I sit up straight, trying to look at the door through the blinding glare. "No! Don't come in."

"I've seen you throw up before, Jared. If you're feeling sick, would you just let me help you?" The door cracks open and I lunge for it, slamming it shut again as the pain spikes. "What the fuck, Jared? Open the door!"

"No. Harper, you need to—" *run. Get away from me. Get out of here. Take the car and leave.* Those are the words I want to say, but all that comes out is, "Just make us something for lunch. We both need to eat."

"Are you sure?" she asks, and I can hear the concern in her voice, and... fuck, I'm concerned too. Every bad thing I've ever read about on the internet is spinning through my head — brain tumors, aneurysms, schizophrenia. Hell, maybe that's what this is. Or split personalities. Or something else, but something bad, something very bad.

Please leave. "Yeah, babe. Food will help."

I want to scream, but I'm in too much pain for that now. It's immobilizing. I can't see anything, can't hear anything except for the weird hum of my brain slowly disintegrating inside my skull. I know I'm soaked in sweat, but I feel so fucking cold. Nothing makes sense, none of this feels real, and the last thought that feels like mine is just two words: *protect Harper.*

The quiet series of knocks on the door pulls my attention away from the mirror, and I stare at the door for a moment before Harper's voice comes through it.

"Babe, you've been in there for like half an hour. I've got sandwiches, and I heated them up in a pan so they're kind of like paninis. No grill marks, but I figured warm food would be better since you said you were cold." She pauses, and I feel my lips tilt up in a smile. I can sense how nervous she is. She's broadcasting it with every wobble of her voice, and I know if I open the door, I'll find her chewing on her thumbnail. "Are you sure you're okay?"

"I'm just fine," I answer, and I can hear her relieved sigh through the door.

"Good. That's really good. I was worried about you." Another pause, because Harper wants comfort. She wants confirmation that everything is going to be okay, but I don't know if that's been decided yet, so I stay silent. "Well... um... I guess come out whenever you're ready."

"I'll be right out, babe." The reply seems to be enough because I hear her light steps moving toward the kitchen. I don't immediately follow her though, instead I turn my eyes back to the mirror. The stubble on my cheeks is filling in, and I know in another day or so I'll have a dark shadow of scruff across my face, which feels more... right. There's an odd shadow under my eyes, and they don't look as clear as I'd like, but I was able to hunt and that's all that really matters.

Well, that, and keeping Harper here.

She'll leave you if you let her. You have to make her yours. Claim her as yours before she chooses another.

The thought is almost like a whisper, brushing against my ear and the inside of my mind at the same time. Something familiar, and yet not, but I know it's the truth. I have to be sure Harper will choose me. Sharing a meal with her will help to calm any concerns she has, and I think I might be hungry. I don't remember eating today anyway.

Turning on the faucet, I splash water over my face and grab the towel to dry off, checking my reflection once more before I open the door and head into the kitchen. Harper is wearing her clothes again, and I chuckle as I look down. "I think I'm a little under-dressed."

Harper grins when she glances at me, her gaze lingering near my hips. "Maybe a bit. Do you still feel cold?"

"Not right now."

"Okay, well..." She laughs a little, picking up the plates off the counter to carry them to the table. "Go put on some clothes anyway. I've got the food ready."

Stepping forward, I catch her arm and spin her to face me. "You don't get to tell me what to do, Harper."

Her brown eyes go wide as she stares up at me, and I tighten my grip on her arm when she tries to pull away. Eventually, she swallows and does her best to sound calm when she finally responds. "I wasn't trying to tell you what to do, Jared. It's up to you if you want to eat naked."

"That's true. It is my choice," I say, leaning forward to press a kiss to her forehead before I let go of her arm. "But I think pants would be a good idea."

"Okay," she whispers, her gaze avoiding me when I offer her a smile. It's not the best reply, but I'll take it for now.

When I head back into the bedroom, a wave of dizziness hits me and I stumble into the bed.

Protect Harper.

Protect.

My stomach twists as the thought pulses behind my eyes like a throbbing headache, and I struggle to remember why I came into the bedroom in the first place.

Clothes. I need to get dressed so we can eat lunch. Harper made lunch for us, and I need to eat.

Nodding to myself, I kneel down beside my duffel bag to pick out clean clothes, but one whiff of myself tells me I shouldn't ruin them before I shower. That leaves me the still damp shirt on the floor, and the jeans and boxers I had on before Harper and I had sex. As I'm shoving the clean clothes back into my duffel bag, my fingers brush against the ring box and I carefully lift it out.

This is why we're here.

My thoughts are all jumbled, making it hard to focus, but I know this is why I brought her out here. This is my family's sacred space, a place meant *only* for family, which is why I wanted to ask her here. It was supposed to mean more because this place, this land, is where my family has been for over a century. We've walked it, generation after generation, passing it down.

Now, this is my forest, and I always knew when I finally brought a girl out here it would be special. She would be special.

And Harper is that and so much more.

The headache pounds again, and I drop the ring box back into my bag and rub at my temple, trying to make it go away. When it continues to thud behind my eye, I shove the box to the bottom of my duffel and stand up to find my dirty clothes.

I'm still dizzy as I gather them off the floor, and it's even harder to focus. I keep staring at the journals on the ground, wondering why Harper would touch them. They're not hers. Not yet anyway. I have to make her a part of the family first.

I have to claim her.

Shaking my head, I rub at the buzzing in my ear before I pull on my jeans and button them. Finally dressed, I look at the lamp on the bedside table, tapping it a few times to see if I can get the weird electric hum to stop — but it doesn't. Picking it up and shaking it doesn't make a difference either, so I set it back down and make a mental note to look for light bulbs. Just in case this one is about to go out.

"Jared?" Harper calls for me, and for some reason her voice grates on me even though I know she's just reminding me that lunch is ready. I try to brush it off, but the irritation lingers along with the buzz in my ears as I head back to the table.

CHAPTER EIGHT
Harper

I'M RELIEVED THAT JARED IS EATING, BUT THE heavy silence is bothering me. He's sick, or at the very least he's not feeling well... but he won't admit it to me. I'm not sure if this is some kind of man thing where they refuse to admit anything is wrong until they're basically too weak to move, or if I'm just overreacting.

I don't think I'm making this up though.

He still looks too pale, and he's eating slowly instead of wolfing it down like he always does. Hell, I've seen him eat a large pizza on his own before, and somehow one sandwich has taken him over fifteen minutes to get halfway through.

"Babe?" I break the silence again and he just

looks up at me, eyes sunken and red, waiting for me to continue talking. "Did you want to go on the hike today?"

"Maybe later," he mutters, and I shift in my seat, glancing out the window at the sunlight. I haven't checked my phone in a while, but I know it's after noon by now.

"Well, how long does the hike up the mountain take? That way we can figure out when we need to leave so we still have daylight when we're coming back down." I try to keep my voice upbeat, encouraging, but Jared just stares at me for a moment before he takes another bite of his sandwich, chewing slowly.

Okay...

"If you don't feel up to it, that's okay too," I offer, smiling just in case he looks at me, which he doesn't. "We can do whatever you're in the mood for, even if that's just hanging out in front of the fireplace and those creepy deer heads."

"They're trophies."

"That's cool..." Tucking one of my legs into the chair, I lean forward on the table. "Are any of them yours?"

"Yes. We always mount the first deer we

take down." His voice is deadpan, weirdly empty, and I hate that he's pulling away from me again. After the sex he seemed so freaked out, and while I wasn't exactly comfortable with what happened, I'd still hoped we could talk about it... but he's made it pretty clear that's not going to be a topic of conversation.

Looking over at the deer heads, I try to ignore the black holes of their eyes. "Which one is yours?"

"The one to the left of the fireplace." Jared turns in his seat, pointing toward the one just off the side of the stone hearth, then he moves his finger further left. "That one is Ollie's."

"So, you only keep the first ones you kill?" I ask, and his arm drops as he faces the table again, but his eyes are on the food instead of me.

"We don't hunt for trophies. We hunt to feed the family, and our friends. It's about providing, not about showing off. It's why the deer are mounted here and nowhere else." He pushes the plate back and suddenly stands up. "I'm going for a walk."

"Oh, okay! I'll come with you." Pushing my chair back, I stand up and follow after him, but he turns to face me, and I freeze.

"You should stay here, Harper." More deadpan tone. He doesn't even sound like Jared when he talks to me like that and I hate it.

"I don't want to stay here. I want to come with you." The words come out a little whiny, but at this point I don't even care. I just want him to stop pushing me away. When he shakes his head, anger flares to life in my chest. "You're not making any sense, Jared! Earlier you were acting like you thought I was going to leave you, and you couldn't stop saying that I'm yours when you were fucking me, but now you don't even want me going on a walk with you?"

"I won't be gone long."

"Then why can't I come with you?" I ask, exasperated by the hot and cold bullshit.

"I... I just want to check the woods. Make sure we're safe to go out." He's looking at the door with a kind of desperation that I don't really understand, but I know he won't give in. At least this time he didn't bite my head off over it.

"Fine. I guess I'll just wait here and watch a movie or something. Or, wait, am I allowed to touch the TV?" Laughing bitterly, I walk toward the couch and throw my hands up. "Before you go is there anything else I'm not allowed to touch in this cabin? Anything that might piss you off?"

"No." Jared shakes his head and opens the front door, and I watch him walk out without even a glance back at me.

"Are you fucking kidding me!" I shout at the door as it closes, but he doesn't come back inside. Growling under my breath, I stomp into the bedroom and strip off my clothes, deciding that a shower is what I need right now.

No, what I really need is for us to just go home.

Jared has been getting weirder and weirder the longer we stay here and I'm over it. As soon as he gets back from his 'walk,' we're going to talk about it. Maybe we can even pack up and get on the road in time to be home before dark.

Whether or not this cabin is important to him, it's definitely not the romantic getaway weekend he'd described it as.

If anything, it's only driving a wedge between us, and I love him too much to let this stupid place tear us apart.

I'm halfway through the original Poltergeist movie when I finally hear the door open behind me. Reaching for the remote, I pause it and stand up from the couch, crossing my arms as Jared walks back inside. He's coated in sweat, looking even worse than he did before he left, and all of my irritation evaporates as I rush over to him. "What the fuck, Jared? Are you okay? What did you do out there?"

"I went for a run," he answers, still deadpan but breathing hard. When he lifts his head to look around the room, he wobbles, and it seems like he's about to pass out on his feet. "I need to sit down."

"Yeah, I think that's a good idea." Grabbing his arm, I help him over to the couch, and while his shirt is soaked with sweat again, I can tell he's cold. "Jesus Christ, Jared. What were you thinking? You already weren't feeling well, and you decide to go for a run in the woods? You're even more pale than you were when you left."

"Had to run," he mumbles, and I roll my eyes as I walk into the kitchen to get a glass of water for him.

"Well, you're not doing that again." Walking back to the couch, I offer the glass of water and the look he gives me is almost... hateful.

"Don't tell me what to do, Harper."

"Are you fucking kidding me, Jared? Something is WRONG with you! You haven't been right since we got here and I'm getting seriously worried about you. I think you're sick and we need to go home."

"NO!" he shouts, shoving himself up from the couch, and I step back as he faces me. "You're not leaving."

"I'm not planning on going anywhere by myself. We *both* need to leave, Jared. We need to go home." Walking around him, I slam the glass on the coffee table, not even caring that water splashes out of it. "If you don't want me trying to take care of you, then stop putting yourself in harm's way. Pay attention to your body, Jared. Something isn't right and if you keep pushing yourself, you're going to get hurt and I don't even know how the fuck to get out of here.

Have you even thought about that? About what would happen to *me* if you'd passed out in the woods on your fucking run?"

"I'd never leave you here. I'm fine."

"You mean you'd never leave me here on purpose, but how would you prevent it if you fell and broke your leg? Or just passed out because you're obviously sick and pushing yourself anyway?" Groaning, I turn away from him to get my shoes from beside the door. "You know what? I don't know what's wrong with you, but I think I'm the one that needs a walk right now. Why don't you take a shower and think really hard about how you're actually feeling."

"Stop telling me what to do, Harper. I mean it." There's a threat in his voice, an actual threat, and if I wasn't already so fucking angry, I'd probably feel scared of him right now... but as soon as I pull on my other shoe, I just rip open the front door.

"Maybe instead of being such an asshole, you should think over what I'm saying to you. I'll be back in a bit."

"You can't leave me, Harper." Jared moves toward me and this time I actually feel a trickle of fear down my spine. "I won't let you."

"That's not your choice right now. I'm going on a walk, you take a shower. That way we can both cool off."

"DAMMIT!" he shouts, turning away from me to grab onto the back of the couch. His fingers dig into the leather so hard that his knuckles turn white and I hold onto the doorknob, afraid to move, even though I'd meant it when I said it wasn't his choice whether or not I went on a walk. "Just... don't leave the clearing. Don't go. I mean... fuck!" I think Jared is shaking, but I can't tell for sure, and my anger starts to fade as concern takes center stage again.

"Jared?" I move a little closer to him, but he tenses up and I stop.

"Get out. Just don't go too far. Don't go where I can't see you. I don't—" A groan rips out of him and he almost buckles, leaning forward onto the back of the couch. "Fuck. Please. Just go outside."

His voice is strained, and I want to help... but I don't know how. Swallowing, I ignore the rush of goose bumps on my skin and pull the door open all the way, keeping an eye on him to see if he tries to stop me. "I'll be right back."

"Go," he growls, and I don't argue. I step outside and pull the door closed behind me, looking up at the evening sun as if there might be some kind of answer in the warm light. There's no answer though, no explanation, no logical reason for why Jared's apparently losing his shit. All I know is that I need to get us out of here. I need to get him help before he drops dead.

I don't know how long I've stayed outside. I should have brought my phone with me, but once I found the little overlook and sat down to look out at the rolling hills of beautiful green trees, my mind just sort of... calmed. It's the first time I've felt any kind of peace since our first night here, and I've probably spent too long sitting here, watching the sun descend as I thought through everything going on with Jared.

He's never been this irritable before. Not even when we've been camping and hiking on less sleep, and I'm confident that he's never talked in his sleep before.

And then there was the sex.

It was more than just aggressive, it was... kind of scary. Of course the orgasms had been spectacular, but even hours later I'm still sore. Before this trip I would have never believed Jared could hurt me, that he'd want to hurt me, but with the cool, clean air on my face and the sounds of birds in the trees.... I can't ignore the little voice in the back of my head that whispers *'be careful.'* In a million years I would have never believed that I could be afraid of him, but I am. The way he's shouted, the way he covered my mouth when I tried to get him to talk to me — and then he basically forced himself on me.

Kind of.

Fuck, why is this so confusing?

Burying my face in my hands, I try to take deep breaths, to think about things objectively... but that only makes it worse. If one of my friends had described their boyfriend doing what Jared did, I'd be lighting a torch and grabbing a pitchfork. It doesn't matter that I ended up enjoying it, or that he *eventually* put on a condom. He shouldn't have done that without talking to me about it first. Whether or not he was irritated with me for looking at his family's journals.

Although, it's not like I didn't want to have sex with him. We'd gone all of Friday without having sex at all, and I had planned to try and seduce him this morning when I found him chopping wood like his life depended on it. But that doesn't excuse it. There are no excuses for how he's been acting, and I have to make that clear to him. I have to make sure he understands this isn't going to be a new normal for us.

And if this is related to some kind of sickness, then we'll get him to a doctor tomorrow and everything will be okay. Everything will go back to normal, and I'll have my sweet, funny, amazing boyfriend back again.

Nodding to myself, I stand up and dust off my jeans and my hands. Taking one more look at the way the light skirts around the mountains in the distance, I turn toward the cabin, prepared to make Jared have a serious conversation with me no matter how pissy he is.

Unfortunately, when I walk in the front

door, I find him passed out on the couch in front of the reinvigorated fire. He's in different clothes, which means he at least listened to me about taking a shower, and I try to take that as a good sign. If he's listening to me again, then maybe I'll have a chance to get all of this shit out in the open when he wakes up.

Grabbing a glass of water, I pick up one of the chairs from the table and carry it over to the TV. Since I'm not supposed to touch the books, and I didn't bring anything to entertain myself with, that means I'll be finishing Poltergeist while Jared takes a nap. I roll my eyes as I grab the remote off the coffee table, remembering how irritated he got when I suggested a nap the day before — but I was right. It's exactly what he needs, and it just proves my point that he's sick. Going for a run when he already wasn't feeling well was stupid even by guy standards.

He's cute when he's sleeping though.

Jared has his arm bent under his head, and his long legs are stretched out as much as they can be on the couch. The slow, even rise and fall of his chest is comforting, because I know he's actually getting some decent rest. The tossing and turning last night probably wasn't very restorative, and even though he was a jerk when I tried to get him a blanket... I still love him. Even when he's being an idiot, or an asshole.

The blanket is still draped over the back of the couch, and I tug it down to lay it over him, and he doesn't even budge. *Definitely sleeping hard.*

Taking a deep breath, I watch him for another minute or so, and I almost feel as peaceful as I did outside. It feels like things might actually be okay, like *we* might actually be okay.

And I want that more than anything.

CHAPTER NINE
Jared

SHE'S GOING TO LEAVE YOU.
Claim her.
Make her yours before it's too late.

The weird whispers linger in my head as I wake up, talking over each other in a clatter that only makes my headache worse. Just leftovers from the strange dream I was having. Out in the woods, hunting for something that I couldn't find, which isn't possible. In these woods, *my* woods, I always find what I'm looking for. It's just another weird thing about my family, or at least this property.

I've only gone hunting in other places a few times, and while I always went home with something, it was never as easy as it has been here. In my forest the land seems to know me, seems to know what I need, and it makes sure I get it. Just like it has for my father, and my grandfather, and every Loxley that has walked these woods for generations.

Which is why the dream is making me uncomfortable.

I try to take a breath and sit up, but I end up coughing, my chest aching as I try to stifle it when I see Harper turn over on the floor. She's got her head on one of the pillows from the bed, and a blanket that's only pulled up to her waist now. Shaking my head, I toss off the blanket she obviously put on me before she made the little pallet on the floor just so she could be close to me. Scooping her off the floor, I adjust my hold on her so she's secure against my chest before I carry her into the bedroom. She smells amazing, the hint of her shampoo mixed with the fresh air outside and the vague hint of the fire that's still smoldering in the living room.

I love her so fucking much, and I know the lingering thoughts in my brain are wrong. Harper wouldn't leave me. I know she wouldn't.

When I lay her on the bed, I have to tug the

sheet out from under her so I can pull it over her legs. She wrinkles her nose in her sleep, immediately rolling onto her side to curl up, and I feel a sense of pride that I was able to take care of her. She would have been so sore in the morning if I hadn't woken up to move her.

What time is it anyway?

Looking around the floor for my phone, I can't see it in the dark, so I crouch down to feel around with my hands where I saw it last. I know it was plugged in near my duffel bag, but when I trace my hand over the wall, I find the socket empty. My charging cable isn't plugged in anymore... what the fuck? Standing up, I glance at Harper again before I move to her side of the bed where the moonlight makes it easy to find her phone. Right next to the bed.

I tap the screen to wake it up and I'm frustrated that it's only a little after eleven. I don't even remember falling asleep, but I must have been tired to pass out like that — and now I'm wide awake. *Great.*

Heading back into the living room, I jab the fire a few times with the poker, getting the smoldering coals to burn hot again before I add a few more logs. The cabin still feels so fucking cold to me, and as I crouch in front of the fire the puff of smoke makes me cough again, only this time I can't stop. My lungs hurt from the wracking coughs, and I sit down on the floor just to give myself a break. When I finally stop, my next breath is a wheeze, and I can feel my pulse pounding behind my eyes. Each beat of my heart feels like a drum banging on the inside of my skull, making the headache worse.

Is she worthy?

Do you want to make her yours?

I shake my head, grabbing at my hair as the weird thoughts flicker through my mind. They don't feel like me... but I know I want Harper in my life.

Take her.

I'm off the floor and standing in the doorway to the bedroom before I even remember moving. She's curled up exactly where I left her, hair fanned out beside her in the moonlight, the glow of it highlighting her profile. She's beautiful... and she's probably cold. Turning around, I grab the stuff off the floor and carry them to the bed. I leave the pillow next to her, because I don't want to wake her up, but I shake out the blanket and drape it over her — just like she did for me.

This is why we'll work as a couple in the long run.

These little things are what can make a marriage work. I saw it growing up with my mom and dad, and I know that Harper sees it too.

There's a strand of hair over her face, and I reach over to brush it out of the way, but my hand stops in mid-air when I see a dark stain on the sheets. Grabbing her shoulder, I turn Harper onto her back and feel a dizzying wave of panic crash into me. There's a cut across her throat, and blood. So much blood. It's everywhere and she's not moving, she's not even breathing, and suddenly I can't breathe either.

My knees buckle as another piercing headache makes my skull feel like it's being split in two, but inside the pain there's a hum and a voice whispering. The same voice from my dream.

Make her yours, or kill her.

She can't leave unless she belongs to you.

I want to scream 'no' but when I try to make

my voice work, I just start coughing. Bracing my hands on the floor, I feel like I'm choking, the coughs even worse than before, and then everything goes dark.

CHAPTER TEN
Harper

I WAKE UP IN BED INSTEAD OF ON THE FLOOR, AND it's a little disorienting. Especially when I look over and realize that Jared isn't in bed with me. If he woke up in the night and moved me, why wouldn't he just climb in bed with me?

Rolling over, I lean over the side of the bed to check the time on my phone, but I don't see it connected to the charging cord. Sighing, I stretch, feeling my back pop in the most wonderful way before I get up and tilt my head from side to side as well. Another series of pops relieves more tension. I'm not sure how long I slept on the floor, but it was clearly long enough to leave me a little stiff.

Now I just need to find my phone.

Scanning the floor, I try to figure out where it could have gone, and I crouch down to look under the bed and the bedside table, but it's not there either. *Strange.*

"Jared?" I call out, finally noticing the bedroom door is shut. When I open it, I expect to find him on the couch again, but it's empty. Groaning, I grab my shoes and pull them on, muttering to myself. "I swear to God, if he's chopping firewood again, I'm going to lose my shit."

Just as I get to the back door, I hear the front door open and I turn around to see him coming inside. He looks... a lot better. There's color in his cheeks again, and a big smile on his face. "Hey, babe! I was just going to come wake you up."

"Hey, how long have you been up?" I ask, walking over to him as he tries to stomp the mud off his boots on the steps.

"Not sure, a few hours maybe?" He shrugs and smiles at me, reaching for my hand to pull me close enough to kiss. A huge wash of relief floods through me as his warm lips touch mine. *He's okay. He's back to normal.* "I know it's our last day, but I was hoping you'd still like to take that hike later?"

"That would be great, babe." The stupid smile won't leave my face, but I don't even care. I'm so fucking happy that he's okay, that he's acting like *my* Jared again. "Oh, did you see my phone this morning? It's not on the charger."

"No, but I might have kicked it when I was carrying you to bed last night." Grinning, Jared steps inside the cabin and walks over to the kitchen to fill up his water bottle. "Someone decided it was a good idea to make a bed on the floor."

"I was worried about you. I didn't want to leave you alone in the living room in case something was wrong."

"Well, I feel much better today. Maybe I just needed a good night's sleep." He winks at me, and I feel the warm flutter in my chest return. I don't have any fucking idea what's been going on the last few days, but I'm relieved it's over. As I lean against the kitchen counter, I notice the dirt on his pants and the mud still caked on his boots and I laugh.

"What have you been doing out there this

morning? Rolling around in the dirt?"

Jared laughs, looking down to try and dust off his pants, but it's useless. It's embedded in the fabric and only a good wash is going to get them clean now. "I wasn't rolling around in the dirt, I was just checking the area, but I found something cool I want to show you."

"What is it?" I ask, refilling my glass from the night before to take a drink.

"That would be a spoiler, and you know how much I hate those." He grins at me, and I can't help but smile back. It's just so fucking nice to have him back to normal.

"Okay, fine. I just need to brush my teeth and put my hair back up. Did you already eat breakfast?" I ask as I head toward the bathroom, and he follows me, lingering in the doorway to watch me as I start brushing.

"I had a bar. Didn't feel like cooking a whole meal this morning, I wanted to get outside."

Popping the toothbrush out of my mouth, I look over at him. "You definitely seem to be feeling better today. Back to normal?"

"I'm all good, babe. Never felt better." Leaning into the bathroom, he smacks my ass.

"Hurry up! I want to show you the woods."

Laughing, I hurry through my routine, stopping into the bedroom to add some sunscreen while I do one more sweep for my phone. I even dig in my duffel bag for it, but it's not there... which doesn't make sense. Phones don't just walk away. Moving to Jared's side, I notice his charger isn't even plugged in anymore, but just as I crouch down beside his bag to look for it, I hear his voice from behind me.

"Are you snooping, detective?"

"No!" I laugh a little as I stand up. "I'm just trying to find my phone, or yours. I can't find either of them. Did you move them somewhere?"

"Why would I do that?" Jared claps his hands together and turns back into the living room. "Come on, come on! You're being so slow this morning."

Sighing, I scan the room again, but I'm not sure where they could be. "Fuck it, I'll look when we get back."

"Harper!" he calls out, and I groan.

"Oh my God, I'm coming!" I raise my hands up as I walk into the living room, heading for the kitchen. "You have zero patience today."

"We've only got today to see everything. I don't want to waste it."

"Right," I reply, ignoring the urge to point out that *he* was the one who has been preventing us from exploring the woods or going on the big hike up the mountain. There are still some things we need to talk about, but I don't want to pick a fight. Not when he's finally in a good mood, and we're both actually enjoying our time together again. Grabbing a granola bar, I tighten my ponytail and turn around to find him slinging his bow over his shoulder. "Are we going hunting?"

"Just a precaution, babe. Same reason I've got this." Jared lifts the leg on his jeans, and I see an ankle holster for a pistol. Guns still weird me out, and it must show on my face because he sighs and walks over to me, cupping my chin to tilt my face up. "It's better to be safe than sorry, right? Just try not to think about it."

"That's easier said than done," I reply, trying to suppress the uncomfortable feeling rolling like a shiver down my spine.

"You trust me, don't you?" he asks with a

smile, but up close there's something off about it. Like it doesn't reach his eyes. "Babe?"

Shaking off the feeling, I nod. "Of course."

"Good, then let's goooo! The weather is perfect." Jared practically bounces out the door, and I follow him, making sure the door is shut tight behind us. "See? Isn't it beautiful out here?"

"It really is," I reply, taking a deep breath of the fresh air as we walk toward the tree line. "I sat out at the overlook for a while yesterday. You were right that the views are incredible."

"I love this place. Everything about it is so pure. No loggers tearing the trees down, building muddy tracks through the forest. There's just nature, the same way it was hundreds of years ago." Jared tilts his head back, looking up at the sky for a moment. "This is how the world was always meant to be."

"It is amazing, but I think you'd miss the internet after a while." I laugh, but Jared doesn't respond at all as he leads the way through the trees. "That was a joke, babe."

"I know." He turns to smile at me over his shoulder, and then we start climbing up a rise.

The ground is a little wet in places, and I wish I'd stopped to put on my hiking boots before we'd left.

"How far out are we going?" I ask, grabbing onto a small tree to steady my footing as I navigate the way up, trying to step in the same spots that Jared does.

"Just a little farther."

"Okay... well, should I head back and grab my boots?" The words are barely out of my mouth when he turns around and grabs my arm with an intense look in his eyes.

"No. You need to stay with me." His grip loosens a bit, and then he smiles again and lets go of me. "It's really not much farther. I promise."

Nodding, I rub the spot he grabbed. "All right. Lead the way."

"This is going to be so much fun. You'll see," he says as he turns to continue up the rise, and I follow him, but I drop back a little so that I'm not as close as before. I want to believe that everything's okay, but there's something still off with him. I'm glad he looks better, and he doesn't seem sick anymore, but I'm getting the same feeling I got before we came out to the cabin. He's keeping something from me, a secret, and I don't think it has to do with something 'cool' he found in the woods.

I'm so focused on not slipping or tripping over the hidden rocks and roots in the underbrush that I don't realize how long we've been walking until I feel sweat trickle down my back. Even with the cool air, the effort of the hike is still way more than I expected when he said he wanted to show me something quickly. Stopping, I turn around in a circle, trying to spot a landmark, but the trees are too dense here.

"Tired already, Harper?" Jared asks from ahead, and I hear him chuckling in the quiet of the woods.

"No, I'm not tired. Just trying to figure out where we are."

"Don't worry about that, the place I want to show you is just down this ridge." He beckons me after him with a wave of his hand, and even though that uncomfortable feeling is waking up in my stomach again, I follow him.

There's a flat area of land at the base of the ridge, and it looks like someone tried to line it with flat stones at some point. They're overgrown with moss now, and there's leaves and dirt scattered everywhere, but it's clear that this isn't natural. It was man-made, done by someone on purpose. "What is this place?"

"Honestly, I have no idea." Jared laughs, walking toward the center. "But I think it was meant for my family... or made by my family."

"How do you know?" I ask, but he's already tapping his boot on a stone in front of him. It's the only space that's been brushed clear.

"Come see." He holds out his hand, and my curiosity draws me closer, but I don't take his hand. Instead, I crouch down to see the carvings on the stone better. They've been worn by time, but I recognize it almost instantly.

"It's your family crest."

"Bingo!" Jared claps his hands together. "Look at that, you're so clever, Harper. My little detective."

Standing up, I move away from him. His tone is cruel, mocking, and I don't like the way he's looking at me at all. It's in his eyes. There's something off with his eyes. "Thanks for showing me this, Jared. Let's head back to the cabin now, okay?"

"Oh, Harper... do you really think that's what's going to happen next?" His smile sends a chill down my spine, and I take another step back, but he matches me. "You're getting ahead of me, babe. It's not time to run yet."

"This isn't you, Jared. There's something wrong with you, and we can get you help," I say, taking another step back. "We just need to go home."

"Something wrong with me?" Jared laughs, spreading his arms wide as he tries to close the gap between us. "Babe, I've never felt so *right*. Everything is so clear out here. Everything just makes sense."

I'm moving steadily backward, curving in a circle, because the ground rises all around us, and there's no way I'll be able to outrun him up an incline. I need to keep him talking, I need to get him to snap out of this. "What do you mean? What's clear?"

"You. Me. *Us*." Jared brings his hands together in a loud clap, interlocking his fingers as he stares at me with a disturbing intensity. "That's what has been wrong all this time,

Harper. We've been together, but we haven't been united. You haven't really been mine."

"What are you talking about, Jared? You're not making any sense." I shake my head, taking another few steps away when he moves closer again, holding out his clasped hands like they somehow explain the words he's saying.

"You're not mine, which means you could have been with anyone. *Anyone* could have taken you from me."

"What?" I sputter over my words as I realize what he's implying. "You think I cheated on you? You really think I'd ever fucking cheat on you?"

"It's possible, isn't it?" He drops his hands to his sides, shrugging a shoulder which lifts the bow a little higher. "I mean... you're not mine, and you're beautiful, wealthy. We both know your family wishes you were with someone closer to your *social standing*."

"My family doesn't give a shit about—"

"DON'T LIE!" Jared roars, and then he raises his hands up, a low, strange chuckle passing his lips. "Sorry, I just really fucking hate it when you lie to me, Harper. We both know your mom thinks I'm trash, and that your dad thinks I just want to get my hands on whatever fucking inheritance you're going to get."

I shake my head, but I can't find my voice now. Arguing with him about my family isn't going to get me out of this situation, it's only going to piss him off more, and I need to be calming him down. When I step backward again, I almost trip over a loose stone, but I manage to regain my footing, holding my hands up in front of me to try and keep him from getting too close. "Jared... babe, you know I love you. I love you so much, and whatever you think is going on, I swear to you I've never loved anyone but you. I haven't been with anyone else since we met. We *live* together. When would I have ever—"

"I really don't want to listen to your lies, Harper. I chose you, out of everyone we know, I chose *you*. I've never even brought anyone else out here. Not any friends, no other girls. I wanted the person I shared this place with to be special, and the land knows that." Jared looks around, taking a deep breath as that strange smile sits on his face like a mask that doesn't fit quite right. "My forest knows that I want you to be mine, to be a part of my family, and it's shown me how to make that possible."

"Wh-what did it show you?" I ask, even though I'm very sure I don't want the answer.

"I have to follow the old ways." He nods, stepping closer, and I move back faster, trying not to trip and fall whenever my shoe catches on an uneven stone, but he's not slowing down now. "I have to claim you the right way. Here. In my forest."

"Claim me..." My head spins, and I feel my heart racing as I start to understand. "You want to fuck me? In the woods?"

"Oh, it's so much more than that, Harper. I'm sure you'd spread your legs for me, beg for my cock if I told you to, but that wouldn't be enough. Not yet, anyway."

I feel a rush of anger splinter through the panic and fear, and even though I'm still trying to stay out of his reach, all I want to do is slap him. "I'm not your fucking whore, Jared. You think I'd fuck you after all this shit? You're crazy! There is something very wrong with you, and you need to listen to me! I'm saying no. I don't want to have sex out here. I want to go back to the cabin, pack our shit, and go home. Now."

"You're not going home, *babe*." His low, rolling laugh makes me shiver, and I realize how incredibly vulnerable I am. When he fucked me on the bed yesterday, that had been rough, but he wasn't like this. He wasn't this far gone, and I feel very, very sure that I don't want him touching me right now.

"Where are we going then?" I ask, my voice wavering, and I hate that I'm on the verge of tears. I want to be strong right now, I want him to see that I'm strong, but I can feel the burn in my eyes and the shaking in my hands.

"Well, you're going to run," he answers, that dark smile still hovering on his face, and I feel my stomach drop. "I don't really care which direction, and I'll give you a solid head start. It just wouldn't be fair otherwise, since I know the terrain, and I know how to track. What do you think, five minutes?" Jared pulls my phone out of his pocket, and I want to scream, but all that comes out is a broken sound when he suddenly lunges for me and grabs my arm, pulling me back against his chest. His arm locks around my waist, squeezing hard as he unlocks the phone and opens the timer app.

"Please don't do this, Jared. Please," I beg, my voice cracking as the first tears roll down my cheeks. "I know you love me. You don't want to hurt me."

"I do love you, Harper." He leans down and takes a deep inhale in my hair before his lips graze my neck, trailing down to that spot by my collarbone that doesn't do a single fucking thing for me as terrified as I am. "That's why this has to happen. You won't truly be mine otherwise. *This* will bind us together. Forever." He presses a kiss to the side of my head, and then whispers the last part directly in my ear. "If you survive."

"Jared..." I whine, but he just laughs as he sets the timer to five minutes, then he turns us and points in a direction.

"The town is about twenty miles that way, not that you'd ever make it that far."

"Please, please don't do this," I babble, sniffling and crying as he squeezes me tighter in some fucked up version of a hug.

"Here's the good news, Harper. If you make it off the property, I'm pretty sure I won't be able to follow you. *Maybe*." He laughs, nuzzling against my hair. "I'm honestly not sure how this works. I've never done it before."

"You don't have to do this at all, Jared," I whisper, and he grabs my arm and spins me away from him in some fucked up dance move made for this nightmare.

"I do, though. I want you to be mine, and there's only one way to make that happen. I have to catch you and claim you for myself. Inside and out. Blood and bone." He suddenly flinches, rubbing at his eye with the heel of the hand not holding the phone. "Ahh, fuck. I thought that was over with."

"What? What was over?" I ask, just trying to buy time at this point.

"Nothing important. My head is still adjusting to all this, but it's not a big deal. It just wants me to tell you that you really, *really* don't want me to catch you." Jared tilts his head, smiling again, and I know it's not him. It's something else, *someone* else wearing his face. "Oh, and one more thing. Time to run."

Jared lifts the phone and taps the start button with his finger, and for a moment I'm frozen, fear and disbelief paralyzing me.

"RUN!" he shouts, and I take off. Instinct driving me up the ridge in the direction he pointed. I have to half-crawl because it's so steep, my feet slipping because my sneakers don't have enough grip on them for this loose ground, but eventually I make it up to the top and I do exactly what he told me to. I run.

As hard as I can, I push myself, leaping over roots and rocks. When I trip and fall the first time, I don't even stop to see what damage I did, I just shove myself off the ground and keep running. I don't know what's wrong with Jared, and I don't know what he plans to do to me — all I know is that I can't let him catch me.

I can feel it in my bones... if I let him catch me, I'll never get him back.

And I don't know what will be left of me when he's done.

CHAPTER ELEVEN
Jared

I'M IN NO RUSH TO CHASE AFTER HARPER. I TOLD her I'd give her a head start, and I meant it.

She's going to need it anyway.

I'm faster than her on a normal hike. I've got a longer stride, more experience, and I definitely know these woods better than her. This is *my* forest, which means I already have an unfair advantage in too many ways. Five minutes isn't going to really matter in the long run. With the clatter she made taking off into the trees, there's going to be plenty of broken branches and disturbed underbrush for me to find her.

It's almost going to be *too* easy.

But this is what the land wants from me.

Not just bedding her in the house but putting in the work to claim her as mine. Giving her a chance to escape like a good hunter would. No traps, no tricks. Just her and me, alone, out in the open.

Glancing at the phone, I see she still has a little over three minutes, and so I take my bow off my shoulder and check it. It's a wooden one, simple, without any of the modern compound bow shit. This is just my strength, my skill, and simple physics guiding the arrow.

Setting it aside, I pull off the quiver and check the fletching and the heads on each arrow. I already did it once this morning, but it never hurts to double-check before you hunt down the woman of your dreams.

I unclip the water from my belt loop and take a drink, feeling a little guilty that I didn't offer her any before she took off — but she probably wouldn't have trusted it anyway. I watched her drink water in the kitchen this morning, and she ate the granola bar during the hike, so it's not like I've started her off at a disadvantage. Beyond the unavoidable ones anyway.

The timer on the phone passes thirty seconds

and I stand up to stretch before I pick up my things. When the jingle finally goes off, I can't help but smile, because somewhere out there Harper is running like a beautiful, scared little rabbit. No... not a rabbit. A fox. Those reddish highlights that the sun always brings out in her brown hair remind me of a fox's coat, and I've seen her run before. She's lithe, quick, not a bouncing little mess.

Yes, my little fox is on the run, and now it's my turn to join our game.

I just have to hope she impresses the land enough to live, because I really do love her, and I'd hate to have to kill her.

I've been following the chaotic path left by Harper's flight for about thirty minutes now, and I'm a little disappointed. When we've gone hiking, I've talked to her about how to leave less of a trace behind, but apparently she wasn't listening.

Or the panic is making her forget.

Both are possible, and while I don't want to

judge her too quickly, I'm still thinking about the little whispers from the land. At first I'd thought they were leftovers from a dream, but then they started to come through clearly, laying out what my forest wanted from me, from *us*. It wants me to claim her, to make her mine, but only if she's worthy. This is her test, our test as a couple, and so far… she's not doing well.

Snapping off a broken twig, I scan the ground to see where it's been disturbed, and I feel a smile slip over my lips. There are three distinct paths out of this little fork in the wood, and while a deer passed by here at some point in the early hours of the morning, the pattern of Harper's sneakers is easy to see in the damp soil as they wander in various directions. *Clever girl.* Maybe she was listening after all.

Picking one at random, I follow it a few yards before backtracking and doing the same for the others. None of them seem to abruptly end, and I'm curious how she managed to produce the effect in so little time. Cupping my hands around my mouth, I raise my voice to call out, "Come out, come out, wherever you are!"

I close my eyes and stay completely still,

listening intently for any sounds of my little fox bolting for safety — but I don't hear anything. *Very clever girl.* Chuckling to myself, I shift the bow higher on my shoulder and follow the center trail. It leads off into the woods for quite a ways, before looping back. Close to her original tracks, but through thicker brush so that I didn't notice them off her main trail. When I get back to the fork she's created for me, I tilt my head and listen for the whispers of the land.

When it stays silent, I decide to talk to it first. "She's not doing so bad. This little trick is going to slow me down."

Find her. Catch her. Don't lose her.

The whispers tumble over each other, almost too hard to make out as they overlap, but I understand. It hasn't made a decision about her yet, but it wants me to pick up the pace. "I can do that."

Choosing the path on the left takes me farther out, but eventually it loops back as well, and I'm not in the mood to laugh when I follow the path on the right and end up exactly where I fucking started. *This* is impossible. She had to go somewhere, Grumbling, I backtrack on the main path, searching the trees on either side for a sign of a new path, a *real* trail to follow, not her tricks. I'm over thirty yards back from her little fork in the woods when I see a perfect outline of her sneaker in a patch of muddy ground. As I follow it, I realize she's not heading toward the town — which would have been pointless anyway. No, my girl is heading back to the cabin.

"So smart. You're always thinking, Harper." I know she's nowhere nearby, but I say it out loud anyway. Half for myself, and half for the land if it's listening. Tapping the car keys in my back pocket, I continue tracking her through the trees. If she's hoping to find some way to escape back at the cabin, she's going to be sorely disappointed. I still haven't found my phone, but it's not like hers would have helped her much. There's no reception out here, and even if she did manage to get a call out... where would she ask for help to come? No address. No street names. Nothing but a set of coordinates that I'm very sure she didn't memorize.

The whispers want me to hurry this up, but I'm enjoying the chase almost as much as I'm going to enjoy what happens when I catch her.

Hopping over a log, I start to hum a tune that's been lingering in the back of my mind all morning. *Dum de dum de de dum de dum.* I still can't remember the words, but the tune is clear as a bell, repeating again and again, so I decide to play along. Whistling or humming along with it as I track her down.

At this point, I'm just curious how long my little fox will be able to keep this up.

CHAPTER TWELVE
Harper

My lungs are on fire and there's a stitch in my side that feels like someone jabbed a knife between my ribs and left it there for fun. I stopped crying a while ago, too focused on the ground beneath my feet and the direction I need to keep moving in if I have any hope of finding the road that leads to and from the cabin. Even if I have to backtrack all the way to the goddamn place, at least I'll be able to get out of here. Once I get to it, I'll actually have a fucking chance. The road will be easier than the woods, faster... but I need to find it first.

I have to ignore the pain and the strain in my breathing, because I have to keep moving. If I stop, he'll catch up.

The little circles I sent him on, *if* he fell for them, will only stall him for so long. I don't have any doubt that Jared will figure out where I really went, he's always been good at this shit. My 'king of the outdoors' who is apparently also an insane shot with a bow, and any other weapon he touches — oh, and completely fucking crazy.

Every time the exhaustion starts to get to me, all I have to do is remember the sinister way he whispered in my ear. *If you survive.* As if my life suddenly means so little to him. The tears burn my eyes again, blurring my vision, and I swipe them away roughly, clenching my jaw against the urge to cry again.

No. You will not break down.

Be smart. Get out of here.

Fucking survive.

Pausing behind a thick tree, I lean against it and scan the sky. The sun isn't quite at its peak yet, which means it's still before noon, and it means *that* direction is east'ish. If I knew more about the movement of the sun throughout the year, I'd know better, but I don't. And it's more than a little irritating that I'm sure Jared knows exactly where the sun is at this time of year. Hell, he's been coming out here for years. He probably doesn't even need the goddamn sun to figure out how to get back to the cabin.

Groaning under my breath, I try to remember the direction we headed when we left this morning, then I try to flip it around in my head to estimate which way I should aim my next stupid dash through the woods. I know I'm probably wrong, but I pick a direction and skim the trees, looking for a path that doesn't look as difficult to move fast. It feels useless, but I refuse to give up. I won't be one of those dumb girls in horror movies that fucks up and gets killed for sheer stupidity.

You really, really don't want me to catch you.

The twisted way he said that sends a chill down my spine, and it kicks off enough of my fight or flight instinct to let me push off the tree and start running again. The momentary pause seems to have loosened the vise around my lungs, but it's done nothing for the stabbing pain in my side. I ignore it though. I ignore everything except the next tree I choose as my goal, choosing a new tree as soon as I reach it.

The little mind game has been the only thing keeping me from completely losing it.

One tree at a time. One breath at a time. Putting one more step between me and Jared. *I hope.*

It's past noon, but I haven't found the cabin or the road yet. I fucked up at some point, chose the wrong direction, the wrong tree, the wrong *something* because if I'd been going in the direction I'd tried to go then I would have passed the road at least.

With my luck, I've just been running in circles. Well, not running. For the last hour or two it's been more like a stumbling shuffle, one half-step above zombie. I've completely lost whatever temporary orientation I had earlier, and while I'm grateful I've managed to avoid Jared for this long... I have no idea where I am. I'm thirsty, hungry, bruised, aching, and my clothes are smeared with mud from one too many misjudged footsteps. All I want to do is sit down and give up.

Maybe if my luck turns around one of those bears will find me and end it quickly, but I doubt it.

Jared would find me first.

Honestly, I'm surprised he hasn't found me yet. It's not like I've got the energy for anymore footprint tricks, and when I tried to climb a tree to hide, all I earned was a massive bruise on my leg. A while ago I would have sworn I heard him shouting in the distance. I couldn't make it out, but I went completely still and listened hard for several minutes, waiting for another shout... but it never came.

So, I keep hiking, moving *away* from him, even though I have no idea where he actually is, but at least I'm moving. I'm still trying even though it's taking more and more effort to lift my foot each time I take a step, and my thighs are burning from the constant rise and fall in the terrain. I'm in decent shape, but apparently I should have been working out on the 'running for your fucking life' plan. Who knew I'd need that particular skill set?

I choose another tree and aim for it, lying to my body that I'll rest as soon as I reach it —

but I think it stopped believing me hours ago. Still, I manage to make it and I lean against the trunk for a moment, forcing deep, even breaths in an attempt to stretch out the constant stitch in my side. I've been heading uphill as much as possible because I feel like that's the opposite of what Jared would expect. He'll know how tired I am, and he'd expect me to take the easy path. Downhill.

I refuse to go down easy though.

Digging my nails into the bark, I shove myself away from it and lean into the hill to keep climbing. The light seems brighter all of a sudden and I look up to find myself much higher than the surrounding foothills. The view is... beautiful. An ocean of green trees waving in the breeze, and the sky is a pale blue, marked with wisps of white cloud that drag in long lines like God let a toddler fingerpaint them on the heavens. If I'm going to die here... at least it's pretty.

A harsh laugh slips past my dry lips, but it doesn't sound anything like me.

I don't feel like myself anyway. None of this feels real. I keep hoping it's some terrible nightmare, that any moment I'll wake up in bed with Jared and all of the terrible chaos of the last few days will be nothing but a weird story I tell him over breakfast that rapidly fades from my mind as dreams always do. I don't want to remember this. I don't want to remember the fear, the panic, the exhaustion.

I don't want to remember Jared looking at me like he's excited to hurt me.

I just want everything to feel normal again.

My legs are shaking now that I've stopped for so long, but I have no idea where to go next. Every direction is downhill now, but with the dense trees there's no chance I can see the cabin. Turning, I realize I'm looking at Mitchell Mountain and it's much closer than it is from the clearing around the cabin. Recognizing a landmark should probably be comforting, but it only makes me feel worse. I didn't look at it enough to know what side of the mountain I'm facing, and even if I could somehow figure it out... I'm just that much farther from the cabin. That much farther from the road, and any hope of getting out of here.

Looking back in the direction I came from,

I wonder how far behind me Jared is now. Is he catching up? Did he stop to rest? Is he waiting somewhere comfortable for night to fall so he can track me down when I'm completely exhausted?

Stupid thoughts aren't helpful.

I take a deep breath and put the mountain at my back, deciding that heading directly away from it is better than continuing to move toward it. Going downhill is much easier, but my legs already feel like jelly and I keep tripping, scratching my hands as I scramble to catch myself on branches and tree trunks. When I find a narrow space between two rises, I don't have the energy to climb up the sides, so I just keep walking forward. There's a dense collection of branches and leaves and pine needles gathered here by rain that slow me down, but it's giving me the chance to rebuild some of my energy.

A few minutes later it starts to open up, widening as the rises on either side descend to meet the land again, and that's when I hear him.

He's *whistling*. Like this is some kind of casual stroll through the woods.

Rage and fear spike in equal measures inside

me, and I use the fresh rush of adrenaline to look for a place to hide. There's a fallen branch that has caught a bunch of the random detritus from the forest floor in its branches, and I carefully pick my way over the ground until I'm close enough to crouch down and crawl deeper into the prickly needles. Every muscle twitch seems to make some leaf crinkle around me, and so I wrap my arms around my legs, trying to stay completely still as the whistling gets closer and closer.

Oh God.

I can hear his footsteps, the soft, measured crunch as he keeps pace with the weird little tune he's whistling. I almost recognize it, and then he starts singing in a creepy, too-happy-to-be-hunting-your-girlfriend voice. "If you go down in the woods today, you're sure of a big surprise..."

My breath catches, an icy shiver rolling down my spine as he gets louder. Closer.

"If you go down in the woods today, you better go in disguise..." Jared starts humming again, the disturbing children's song continuing without words, but I don't need him singing the end of 'Teddy Bear Picnic' to know that he's practically right on top of my hiding place. I don't even think I breathe as he walks past me, heading into the ravine from the opposite direction I came from.

Did he lose my trail?

I don't move an inch as I watch him moving confidently over the hidden rocks beneath the dead leaves and dirt. My heart is pounding so hard against my ribs it feels like it's trying to get out, but I refuse to move even when every cell in my body is screaming at me to run.

Don't be an idiot. Don't die because you're stupid. Wait.

Fucking wait.

It feels like it takes an eternity for Jared to disappear around a slight curve, but I stay still. I know I'm going to make a lot of noise getting out of this weird little branch cocoon, and while I'm so tempted to just lay down and rest... I can't risk him giving up and backtracking. If he comes back this way, there's no way he won't see me, and I've already pressed my luck enough when he didn't turn around as he walked past.

He starts singing again, the same lines, and

his voice echoes off the high walls, but I know he's farther away now. Taking a deep breath, I move as gently as possible, flinching at every crunchy leaf and snapping twig under my hands and knees. A rock jabs into my shin, but I bite my lip to stay quiet as I shift my position and continue crawling out of the hideaway that saved my life. When I'm finally able to stand up, I quickly get behind the nearest tree and fight the urge to peek around it. Instead, I angle away from the ravine, moving as quickly as my legs will carry me so that even if he comes back, I'm long gone.

I'm pulling myself up another rise in the land when I hear something and then my leg explodes in pain. I scream before I can bite down on it, collapsing against the tree beside me as I grab for my thigh and my hand comes away with blood.

No, no, no, no.

Raw panic pours through my veins, burning like fire as I look ahead and see a fucking arrow in a tree maybe twenty feet ahead.

"HARPEEERRRRRR!" Jared calls, and I choke on a sob as I try to keep moving, but my leg hurts so fucking bad.

Limping, I force myself to move from one tree to the next, not even caring about the tears anymore. I just wipe them away and keep going, groaning through the pain as the motherfucker starts whistling again.

"You've sent me on quite a hike today, babe," Jared finally says from behind me, and he's way too fucking close. I don't turn my head though, I just pick the next tree and limp toward it, a whine forcing its way through clenched teeth as I finally get to it and lean on it, taking the weight off my leg for a moment. "It's over, Harper."

It's his low laughter that gives me another boost of energy as I wipe my eyes and choose another tree, shoving myself toward it as I shout, "Fuck off, Jared!"

I've only limped a few steps when another arrow flies past me and *thunks* into the tree I was aiming for. Dead-center on the trunk.

"Tsk, tsk, tsk, Harper. Don't make me actually hit you with the arrow this time."

Stumbling to the side, I catch myself against a much smaller tree and finally turn to face him.

He's got the bow drawn, another arrow ready to go... and he's pointing it right at me. Sniffling, I try to stop the tears with a hard swallow before I lift my chin. "Go on. Do it."

"Done with our little game?" he asks, tilting his head away from the bow to smile at me, and I hate that it's Jared's face looking at me like that. That it's his voice speaking to me like this.

"You found me." I lift a hand in the air, using the other one to support myself with the tree. "That means you win, right?"

Jared relaxes the bow, spinning the arrow in his fingers before he casually puts it in the quiver over his shoulder. "I have to be honest, Harper. I'm impressed."

"Go to hell," I growl, and he laughs. It's a big laugh that bounces around the silent forest like the trees themselves are joining in.

"That's my girl. Still so damn feisty." He plucks my phone out of his pocket and glances at it before holding it up. "Almost five and a half hours, Harper. You should be proud. I had faith that you'd make it for a while, but even I didn't expect our little game to last this long."

"So glad I surprised you," I answer, and he

shakes his head, still grinning like this is the best time he's ever had.

"You really did, babe. I mean, that trick you played on me right off the bat with the multiple trails, and *none* of them were right?" He mimes his head exploding, and all I can think of is how much I wish his head would *actually* explode. "That was so damn smart."

I shake my head at him as he chuckles and leans the bow against a bush, taking the quiver off to set it aside as well.

Snapping his fingers, he raises one in the air. "Oh! And going uphill? I have to admit, you had me mixed up for a while with that shit. I had to turn around and figure out when you started going for higher ground." Jared shrugs, rolling his neck for a second before he looks at me again. "Unfortunately, that's where you fucked up."

"Slowed you down, didn't it?"

"Definitely." He nods, unhooking the water bottle from his hip, tilting it back and forth in his hand, and I can hear the water sloshing inside. "But you fucked up because the cabin isn't toward the mountain, babe. You were on track to make it there. Hell, you started to make me nervous that you'd find the road before I found you... but then you turned around and started heading back out. It's like you wanted me to find you."

"You're not Jared. I don't know what you are, but you're not him."

That dark smile slithers over his face just before he tries to look hurt. "But... I thought you loved me, Harper?"

"I love *Jared*. I hate *you*." I spit the words and he drops the sad puppy act, smiling at me again as he walks closer, and all I want to do is try to run, but I know I'm done. I'm bleeding, and I don't know how deep the gash is, but it hurts like hell, and even if I weren't already exhausted I'd have trouble moving in the woods while limping.

I expect him to grab me, to hurt me, but instead he stops a few feet away and holds up the water bottle. "Do you hate me enough to refuse some water? Because, I know I'm thirsty. I mean, I could easily finish this right now, but I figured you might be a little dehydrated after your stroll in the woods."

Between the goddamn grin on his face, and the bullshit tone he's using, I want nothing more than to slap the fucking bottle out of his hands and spit in his face... but I don't think I actually have enough moisture left in my mouth to do it.

"Come on, Harper," he says with mock sweetness, dangling the water bottle closer to me. "You know you want it."

I lunge for it out of desperation, but he yanks it back and I almost lean too far, putting weight on my bad leg. Clenching my teeth against the groan of pain, I grab for the tree again and blink away the tears so I can glare at him.

"Say please for me, babe."

"You're a fucking bastard," I growl, and he shakes his head slowly, a low chuckle floating on the air between us.

"Okay, Harper." Jared unscrews the top and tilts it up, spilling some of the water past his lips as he takes a long drink. Swallow after swallow, and I hate myself for it, but I buckle.

"Fuck, fine! PLEASE! Please let me have the water." I force the full sentence through clenched teeth, but Jared rights the bottle and looks at me over it, just before he tilts his head down and spits the water in his mouth back inside it.

"Here." He holds it out, closer this time, but I don't reach for it. Sighing, he takes another step toward me and shakes it. "I won't take it away this time. Promise."

"Your promises aren't worth shit."

"Just put out your hand, Harper. We're not done yet, and I really don't want dehydration to be what makes you finally pass out." The words come out so calm, so casual, but they make my stomach twist.

I'm afraid. I'm fucking terrified, but even though it's shameful as hell I hold out my hand and he sets the water bottle on my palm. Closing my fingers around it, I immediately bring it to my lips to drink. If he thought that spitting in the water was going to make me not drink it, he's an idiot. I'm so thirsty I would have drunk from the first water source I came across even if I'd watched something pissing in it upstream. It doesn't take long for me to empty it, and I let the last mouthful swish around for a long minute before I finally swallow. When I screw the cap back on, I look down at the metal bottle and shift my hold on it, carefully wrapping my fingers around it.

"Harper... you've been so smart today. Do you really want to start being stupid now?"

CHAPTER THIRTEEN
Harper

"Being smart hasn't helped me much, has it?" I ask, and I'm relieved by how much easier it is to talk now that my throat isn't sandpaper dry. Jared steps closer, and I drop the bottle to my side, keeping it out of his reach.

"I don't know... I'm pretty sure you've impressed the forest by now."

"I don't give a fuck what your stupid fucking forest thinks!" I shout, and he shakes his head slowly, his gaze moving from the bottle in my hand to meet my eyes.

"You should care what it thinks, Harper. It's the reason that arrow just grazed you." Holding his hand out, Jared wiggles his fingers a little.

"Come on, babe. Just hand it to me."

"Come and get it."

His eyes widen for a second, but I'm ready when he lunges at me. He goes to tackle me, but I keep my hand free and bring the bottle down as hard as I can on the back of his head. Blinding pain shoots through my leg when I land on it, amplified when he lands on top of me, but I don't stop. Screaming through the agony, I hit him again and again until he digs his fingers into my thigh, and it hurts so bad my vision flickers and my stomach churns, threatening to return the water.

"Fucking hell, Harper!" Jared shouts, throwing the empty water bottle into the woods as he sits up, feeling the back of his head, and I'm incredibly disappointed when his fingers come away without any blood. "That actually hurt."

"Good!" Rearing back with my good leg, I kick him in the chest, and I know it's only because I caught him by surprise that he falls, sprawled on his back as I grab for the pistol on his leg. I manage to yank his jeans up with one hand, my other brushing against the snap holding it in place, and then his shin comes up, connecting with my mouth and nose in a flash of white-hot pain. The tears are unavoidable now as I hear him cursing, shouting something that I can't make out through the ringing in my ears. All I can do is turn over to my stomach and drag myself forward. Whatever few inches I gained mean nothing when Jared grabs onto the ankle of my bad leg and yanks me back. I scream, in too much pain to do anything except sob as he grabs a fistful of my hair and yanks my head off the ground.

"What the fuck were you going to do with the gun, Harper? Shoot me?!" He's laughing. He's actually fucking laughing as he shakes me, ripping out strands of hair. "What was your plan after that, babe? You had five fucking hours of wandering around out here and you didn't find *shit*! You think you'd do any better bleeding and limping around in the goddamn dark?"

Jared shoves me back to the ground, and I don't even have the energy to catch myself. I just lie there, whimpering as I feel him reach underneath me to undo the button on my jeans.

"I knew you'd fight me. Hell, I was looking

forward to it! But I think you almost cracked my skull open with that fucking water bottle." He blows out a breath, and I know he's leaned closer because he only whispers the next words. "I have a feeling this is going to hurt a whole lot more though."

"Please," I beg, but I barely get it out before he yanks my jeans down. They're stuck to my skin with sweat and blood, and I dig my fingers into the ground and bite down on the scream as he changes his hold and tugs again. My leg is nothing but pain, overwhelming every other sense as it throbs, every beat of my heart trickling out more of my blood to soak the earth. When he finally tears them free, I can't do anything but try to breathe, waiting for the torment to subside.

"You still with me, Harper?" he asks, shoving the hair out of my face as he leans down, a wide smile stretching his lips. "There's my girl. I'm glad you're still awake."

"Don't. Please don't," I whisper, and he smears the tears across my cheek with a stroke of his thumb.

"This is what today's all about, babe. You

and me." Jared slips his thumb between his lips, licking my tears free with a quiet groan. "I really do love the way you taste. Now... let's see what noises you make for me."

Whining, I fist the dirt and leaves under my hands, but even pulling as hard as I can, I don't move more than an inch or two before his hand lands in the small of my back and presses me into the ground.

"Oh no, babe. No more running." He shifts his weight into his hand, pinning me, and the sudden silence in the woods around us makes the sound of his zipper sliding down too loud.

"No!" I shout, but it doesn't sound very strong as my voice breaks with another sob.

"That's the spirit, Harper. Try and fight me," he growls, leaning over me. I expect him to spread my legs, but he doesn't. Jared plants his knees outside my thighs and his cock brushes against my ass. I can't hold back the whine of fear as he rocks his hips, his shaft sliding between my cheeks. When he leans down, I brace for pain, but he goes still. "I'm not going to fuck your ass. Today anyway. That's not how I'm meant to claim you now... but I will have you in every hole. Nod for me."

I nod, trying not to let the relief spread in my chest because I know this isn't really mercy.

"Tell me thank you," he commands, and I feel his hand working between my thighs, his fingers seeking. Jared's forearm presses down between my shoulder blades, crushing me as he grabs a handful of my hair and jerks my head up. "Say it."

"Th-thank you," I whisper, whining when he lets go of my hair and immediately forces two fingers inside. I'm still sore from yesterday, but that ache is nothing compared to my thigh. Even when he adds a third, ignoring that I'm not wet in the least, I know I can handle it.

"See? We're in love, we're having fun, right?" he growls against my ear, pumping his fingers in and out, but when I don't respond at all he rips them free and sits up. "We're going to have so much fun."

I take a deep breath as my ribs are able to expand again, and when I open my eyes, I try to blink away the spots dancing in my vision. The dappled sunlight is blurring between the trees in a gold-green haze, and for a split second I think of how pretty it looks. Then I hear him spit, and even though I know it won't help, I tense. His hand lands on my back again, pinning me to the dirt as he presses his cock against me.

"You're mine, Harper. Inside and out." The first thrust is so hard it moves me across the ground, and I scream because everything hurts at once. He's stretching me too fast, forcing another inch in as I start sobbing again, and every shift of my body only makes my thigh throb.

"Please, please, please..." I mumble into the dirt, digging furrows with my fingers as he slides back and thrusts again, just as hard, and I choke on the cry. It hurts, but I can't even put it into words as he picks up a rhythm.

"This cunt is mine." Jared runs his other hand up my side and back down, squeezing my ass. "This body is mine."

I want to tell him no. I want to tell him he's a monster, a bastard, a fucking asshole. I want to be strong enough to fight him, to claw the skin off his face, but there's not enough left in me to do any of it. Worse, I can feel my body betraying me. Easing the way for him, and his groan as he slides through my early wetness makes me want to escape myself.

"That's right, babe. You like this," he groans, removing his hand from my back to brace it on the ground. "What did you say yesterday? That you'd like if I was a dominant alpha male sometimes?" Jared nips my shoulder, driving in deeper as I stifle a sob. "Well, how am I doing? Dominant enough for you?"

He doesn't wait for me to answer, he just laughs and starts to fuck me harder, the powerful thrusts rocking me against the rough ground, and all I feel for him is hate when the first inkling of pleasure breaks through the wall of pain.

No. No, no, no.

I try to fight it, but there's something about the position he has me in that makes every stroke of his cock hit the right place inside me, and it's like once I'm aware of it... it's all my mind wants to focus on. I swallow the first moan that's more pleasure than pain, and I plead with whatever god might be listening for him to finish before he makes me come — even though the temptation to feel anything other than pain and exhaustion is so alluring.

"Fuck, you feel so good." Jared moans low, the sound ending on a growl as he slows down, driving in as deep as he can go before sliding back just as slow. It's a whole new layer of torture, forcing me to feel every stroke, every inch, stoking the steadily building pleasure inside me. "Yesss... just like that."

When he suddenly pulls out of me, I feel like my desperate prayers might have finally been answered, but then there's only agony again as he flips me onto my back. The pulse from my leg is enough to turn my stomach, only made worse when he bends my knees toward my shoulders. My scream is weak though, and he's back inside me a breath later, fucking me even harder. There's a war going on in my head over chemicals, mixed signals firing between agony and the oncoming bliss. Terror and relief. Panic and acceptance.

"You're so beautiful like this, Harper," he says, and he sounds so much like *my* Jared that it makes my heart break. "Completely and totally mine."

I'm starting to feel light-headed and it's the

first mercy I've felt all day, but as my barriers fall, I can feel an orgasm slowly building inside the confusing haze. He leans over me, but the throb of my thigh is distant as he spreads my legs, somehow stretching me even further with his next thrust.

"See? When you submit to me, I can make you like it," he whispers against my lips, and when he kisses me, I don't have the energy to fight him. I let him claim my mouth, nipping my lip as the buzz of his groan vibrates low in his chest. "I'm going to make you come for me as I fill you up."

Wait... no.

I force my eyes open and my stomach drops when I see the black void staring back at me. There's no green in his eyes, only darkness. Pitch-black and empty. Like marbles. I try to move, weakly pushing at his chest, but he moves my arms and pins them to the ground next to my shoulders, shaking his head slowly.

"No more of that, Harper. I told you I was going to claim you." Jared thrusts hard, picking up the pace again, and I can't look away from the terrifying emptiness of his eyes. "Now, I'm going to breed you. Make you mine inside and out..."

"No," I whine, crying again as I try to pull at his painful hold on my wrists.

"And once you're round with my child, you'll understand this was meant to be. That this was exactly what you needed." He groans, his eyes closing for a moment, and I take the opportunity to clench mine tight, unable to look into Jared's face to see... *that*. "It's what we both need, Harper."

I shake my head, the movement making me even dizzier, but at this point I'd happily pass out just to make it stop.

"Come on, babe. I know you want to come with me."

I don't. I don't want to be here at all. I want it all to be a dream, a horrible nightmare that I'm going to wake up from at any moment, and I'm hoping that the low hum in my ears is the abyss of unconsciousness finally pulling me in.

Except, it doesn't stop.

It gets louder. Buzzing in a strange, high-pitched way that makes my ears feel strange.

"Do you see now?" Jared asks, and his voice

sounds like it's buzzing too. When I open my eyes to look, all I can see is him and a thick fog. It's everywhere, all around us, over us, shimmering in the sunlight that can't quite penetrate it. I breathe and I can feel it moving over my lips, the cool, tingling texture of it rolling down my throat, filling me up, and when I breathe it out, I'm humming.

"What..." I try to ask what's happening, but the sensation is building, as if every cell in my body is suddenly buzzing at the same frequency as the sound. The next time Jared thrusts it rebounds across my nerves, scattering light inside me, and all I can do is gasp, pulling in more of the strange mist.

"You're mine now, Harper. Forever," he whispers, and I can't even focus enough to remember why I was afraid. There's no pain, no exhaustion, just an infinite hum and a rising tide of pleasure that swells every time he fills me. It's perfect bliss, and a promise of ecstasy if I just give in.

Relax. Open. Accept him.

It seems so easy. A whisper in my mind that makes my muscles go slack, releasing the last of the fear just before my back arches and I feel the friction of each thrust with perfect clarity. Jared's skin is warm against mine, his lips brushing my neck as he whispers my name over and over, and I try to lift my hips to meet his, but it's hard to move. His fingers wrap around my hip to keep me still, and I melt into his kiss, our tongues brushing as I moan, the tension building inside me until I can't handle it anymore.

The orgasm is explosive, a riotous burst of light behind my eyes in a hundred colors that fills my bloodstream and shatters me into a million pieces of electric euphoria. As if I've pulled him over the edge with me, I feel Jared thrust deep, his cock kicking as he fills me with jets of heat, a low growl echoing in my ear as I sink into an endless sea of peace.

No pain. No fear.

Just blissful, perfect nothing.

The world is wrong when I start to wake up.

My head is pounding, and I hurt everywhere. I hurt so much. A croaked cry slips past my lips as I force my eyes open, too weak to lift my head. There's skin, and feet, and ground, and I'm pretty sure I'm upside down.

"We're almost home." That's Jared's voice, but it doesn't explain anything.

It's hard to think, like the worst hangover I've ever felt, but slowly I start to put things together. Jared is carrying me over his shoulder, and I'm a thousand points of pain held together by skin and bones. Pain that Jared caused.

"Down," I whisper, my voice slurring over the simple word, but he just keeps walking even though every step sends a ripple of agony spreading out through my body. "Please."

"You can't walk, Harper. That's why I'm carrying you."

The reboot happening inside my skull is taking its sweet time, but memories are starting to flicker through. Him telling me to run, the endless forest, the exhaustion, and then the arrow. *I'm bleeding. Oh God, how long have I been bleeding?*

As if in an attempt to answer, when I lift my head, everything swims. It's not good. None of this is good, and I know I'm not safe with Jared.

He hurt me. Shot me, and then hurt me again. On the ground, face down in the dirt.

"DOWN!" I shout, trying to move, but Jared just tightens his hold on my legs which makes my stomach flip-flop as a fresh wave of torture steals all the air from my lungs on a cry.

"You have to stop struggling. I've been carrying you for a while, and that's *after* I tracked you for over five hours. Give me a break, okay?" He sounds amused, like he thinks this is funny, and I'm about to try and get down again when I see the ground change to the thin grass and old gravel of the clearing. "Almost inside."

"No..." I whine, but he ignores me as he flips me upright again, catching me against his chest to steady me at the base of the steps to the front door.

"Figured we should do this the right way." Jared grins and leans down, scooping me into his arms. My scream chokes off as he adjusts me and a second stab of agony overwhelms the first. "Have to carry you over the threshold, right?"

"Please don't hurt me," I beg, and he just looks down at me in his arms like I've just told him I love him.

"Here we are!" he announces, bending to turn the doorknob before he kicks it open and carries me inside as he mimics the wedding march. "Dum, dum, de dum!"

I gasp in pain when he lays me on the couch, but I'm just relieved that he's not touching me anymore. I can remember all of it, every horrible thing until I blacked out while he was still fucking me. "Jared... I need to go to the hospital. Please, you have to—"

"You don't need anyone except me now, Harper. You're mine."

Shaking my head, I look down at my legs and realize his shirt is tied tight around my thigh, soaking up my blood. Not that it's enough to keep me alive, and I try my best not to think about the kind of infections I might be contracting from all the dirt embedded in the gash. "No, Jared. I'm not okay right now. Do you understand? You shot me with a fucking arrow!"

"It was a graze, babe. I just needed to slow you down, and I made it up to you, right?" Grinning, he sits on the edge of the couch, catching my arm easily when I try to hit him.

"Harper, you felt it too. I saw you. You connected with the forest and then... *fuck*. You came so hard. Your pussy clenched my cock like a vise."

"No, I didn't connect with the forest. That's not *real*, Jared." I'm trying to get through to him, but there's not a single hint of awareness in his eyes. He just pats my hand before he suddenly stands up.

"Hold on! I know what we're missing." I watch as he rushes into the bedroom, and all I can feel is panic, because I don't think he's planning on getting me help.

This can't be real.

I'm going to fucking die in this stupid cabin with my batshit crazy boyfriend, and no one even knows where I am.

"Harper, you have no idea how wonderful this is," he says as he walks back into the living room wearing a goofy grin that I used to think was cute. A lifetime ago, before he lost his mind and tried to kill me. "I thought I needed to do something special, something *perfect*, but I just didn't know what I was waiting for. It was *this*. I was waiting for this, for us to come here together so the land could accept you. That means you're a part of me, a part of my family. We're bound together for life, and now I can finally give you this."

Jared lifts a small box, holding it toward me as he opens it, revealing a sparkling engagement ring.

Tears well in my eyes as pieces of a puzzle I didn't know was there finally click into place. *This* is why he was acting so weird before this trip. It wasn't about the goddamn cabin, or some secret hike up a mountain... he wanted to ask me to marry him. It's just another level of cruelty in this nightmare, because I would have loved the beautiful ring if he'd given it to me yesterday, or last week, or a fucking year ago — but not now.

"You can't be serious," I whisper, and his brows pull together, his smile dissolving as he looks down at the ring and then up at me again.

"It's a ring," he says, like it's some kind of explanation, as if I don't already know that it's a goddamn ring.

"I know it's a fucking ring, Jared! Why the hell are you trying to give it to me right now? I'm bleeding on your fucking couch! You HURT me!" Grabbing onto my head, I bite down on a scream, feeling like I might be joining him in lalaland pretty soon if the world doesn't start making sense again fast.

"You have to wear it. It's how everyone knows you're mine." He plucks it out of the box and I just stare at him.

"No, Jared. NO! Can you seriously not understand that word?" I shout, leaning closer to him. "You're fucking crazy!"

"No, this is how it's meant to be. You're mine now, Harper, and we're going to start a family, and you have to wear my ring." Jared grabs my hand, but I'm not a match for his strength as he forces the ring onto my finger. "You're my wife."

I'm about to argue when the ring feels like it's burning me. I barely have time to gasp when there's a terrifying rush that makes me sick to my stomach for a moment before it disappears as suddenly as it came — and then Jared collapses.

He starts shaking violently, and instinct takes over as I shift to the floor beside him, trying to remember what the fuck you're supposed to do for someone having a seizure. Desperate, I wrap my hands around the back of his head, trying to stop him from banging it against the wood, but I jump back when he opens his eyes and they're pitch black.

His eyes.

They looked just like that when he was on top of me. It's one of the last things I remember before I blacked out, and the fear is unavoidable as I scramble away from him, my back pressed to the couch as he finally goes still.

And then I see smoke coming out of his mouth. Except it's not smoke. It's too... transparent, too shiny. It's like mist pouring out of him and fading through the wood floor, and what starts as a trickle turns into a rush. Covering him, expanding outward, and I pull myself up onto the couch to avoid it touching me, but I start coughing anyway. The air tastes strangely sweet, in the most horrifying way, and as another wracking cough makes my ribs ache, I feel something cold on my tongue... and mist puffs out of me with each subsequent cough.

Impossible. This is fucking impossible.

If I could get enough air in to scream between the coughs, I would, but by the time I finally stop I'm in too much shock to do anything except watch as the last silver tendrils coil out of Jared's mouth.

Staring at him, I feel things in my head aligning, shifting, and I remember the mist in the woods. It was everywhere, and I *breathed it in*. And then I did come, I did... but it wasn't me. Not really.

It didn't feel like me.

I can't stop shaking, and I know I should check on Jared because he hasn't moved for several minutes. I'm not even sure if he's breathing, and I'm starting to wonder if he's dead when he suddenly gasps, sitting up straight.

"HARPER!" he shouts, and his eyes are wide, panicked, but they're not black anymore. His face crumples in pain, a choked cry as he turns over, bracing his hands on the floor just before he starts to throw up.

What. The. Fuck.

Jared's eyes may not be black anymore, but the stuff he's throwing up on the floor definitely is and based on the sounds he's making it seems to hurt... but I don't move closer to him. I can't make myself, even though I'm more than a little worried about everything happening.

I'm still afraid of him, and I don't know which version of him is with me now.

CHAPTER FOURTEEN
Jared

I THINK BATTERY ACID IS POURING OUT OF ME. I don't actually know what battery acid looks like, but I'm relatively sure it feels *exactly* like this. My throat is on fire, my stomach feels like I ate a few dozen lightbulbs, and I can't stop shaking.

Another wave of the disgusting shit wells up in my throat and I throw up again, but then it seems to slow. After a few more minutes of shaking on my hands and knees, one last bubble of it hits the back of my throat and I do my best to spit everything out. It's solid black, completely dark, and yet somehow the wood is absorbing it without changing color at all. I try to focus on breathing and not the uncomfortable burning that seems to be everywhere at once. I can't think straight at all, but a single thought is running on repeat in the chaos.

Protect Harper.

The words clang like a warning bell inside me, and I wipe my mouth on my arm as I sit down on the floor, determined to find her, to keep her safe. When I finally lift my head, relief flashes through me for a brief second when I see Harper on the couch, but then all my hope disintegrates as I actually look at her. She's curled up at the farthest edge of the couch, streaked with dirt and blood, and I wish more than anything that I didn't recognize my shirt tied around her leg, soaked in even more blood.

I failed her.

Pain lances through my skull, my head pounding, but I keep my teeth clenched tight against the urge to scream as images, *memories* pour into my mind. Sorting and filtering until I have a complete and horrifying understanding of exactly why Harper looks like that.

I didn't just fail her. *I did this to her.*

If there was anything left in my stomach, I'd be throwing it up, but there's nothing. Panic hits me hard in the chest and my lungs go tight. I can't breathe, I can't look at her, and as I shove myself backward, putting more space between us, I have the very clear and decisive urge to put the fucking gun in my mouth and pull the trigger.

But... I can't. Not yet anyway.

She's still bleeding. She needs a fucking hospital, and since I made absolutely sure to wound her right leg, she can't even drive herself away from here. Another flash of her under me in the woods shows up front and center in my mind and I cover my face with my hands, rocking on the floor as the memory plays in my head like a horror movie that I can't turn off. "Oh God... I'm sorry. I'm so sorry."

"Jared?" The way she says my name, so nervous, so fearful, just drives the horror deeper. I can't even respond to her. I don't *deserve* to speak to her.

"I'll get help. I—" My words choke off in my chest when I look up at her again. There are scratches on her face, bruises *everywhere*, and I keep hearing the way she screamed. Over and over again. Scrambling to my feet, I stagger to the side when my head swims, but I manage to catch myself on the hearth and stumble in a wide arc around her and into the kitchen. I remember where the first aid kit is, under the sink, and I drop to my knees in front of it, not giving a fuck how much it hurts to move right now. When I rip the cabinet open, I don't just find the large box of first aid supplies... Dad's satellite phone is there too. Grabbing both of them, I move to the far end of the couch, keeping as much distance between myself and Harper as I can. Setting the kit on the coffee table, I move backward to the bedroom. "I am so sorry, Harper. I... I'm going to get you help. I promise."

"Jared, wait!" she calls after me, but I shut the bedroom door and lean against it.

I can't look at her. Every glance pulls another memory into the front of my head, and I can't focus on that right now. I have to get her help, and as the satellite phone powers on, I manage to walk to the bed and sit down before I hit the floor. I feel weaker than I can remember. My muscles are burning, exhausted, it still hurts to breathe, and my hand won't stop stinging. The little screen on the phone lights up and before

I even realize what number I'm dialing, the phone is ringing.

"This is Charlie." My dad's voice coming over the line has me speechless. *How the fuck do I tell him what I've done?* I hear road noise in the background, and I know he's in his car, probably running some errand for my mom, or Ollie, or Addison. "Hello?"

"Dad," I whisper and my voice cracks, my chest burning from the effort of holding back the sudden swell of emotion.

"Jared? Is that you?" The concern in his tone makes me groan because I'm not the one he needs to be worried about.

Clearing my throat, I sniff hard and try to sound less like an utter fucking train wreck. "Yeah, Dad. I... I did something bad."

"Okay..." His voice drops, and I remember it from a thousand 'serious' conversations we've had over the years. "Tell me what's going on, Jared. Are you still at the cabin?"

"Yeah, I am." I feel sick again because I know that after this he'll never look at me the same again. He'll never love me the same — and how could he?

"I need you to tell me what happened. Whatever it is, we'll figure it out, okay? Just talk to me."

"I brought Harper out here with me. I was going to ask—"

"You did WHAT?" My dad switches from serious concern to pissed off and panicked so fast that I can't even respond before he's talking again. "Jared, tell me what the hell happened. Did you— shit, did you do something to her? Did you hurt her? How many times have I told you that you aren't allowed to bring *anyone* out there?!"

My head is spinning, confusion and guilt battling it out until all that comes out of my mouth is, "You knew?"

"What did you do, Jared!" Dad shouts, and I feel twelve years old again, only the consequences to this are a lot worse than being grounded from the Xbox. "JARED!"

"I hurt her, Dad," I whisper, and before I even realize it's happening, I'm crying. Scrubbing at my eyes as my stomach twists into knots because I can imagine the disappointment on his face, the disgust, and I don't blame him.

I hate myself.

"Jesus Christ, Jared. Did you think I was just being an asshole when I told you to never bring anyone out there? It's the rules! The family rules, you know that!" He sounds more panicked than angry, but I just nod even though he can't see me.

"I know, Dad. I'm sorry." My voice cracks and I try to swallow past the ache in my throat. "I'm so fucking sorry."

"Okay, first things first, is she..." *alive?* He leaves the last word unspoken, but I know that's what he wants to know, and it kills me that he thinks I'm capable of that... but, apparently, I am. I'm capable of so much worse.

"She's alive, but she's hurt. Bleeding. I... I caught her thigh with a broadhead, and—"

"You shot her with an arrow? Jesus Christ, Jared!" Dad shouts, cutting me off before I can even tell him the worst of it. "I thought my dad was crazy. Shit, I thought he was just superstitious, talking about rules and curses and consequences."

"Wait, what?" Sitting up straight on the bed, I'm shocked that my dad is talking about my grandfather at all. The man died when I was seven and we never spent much time around him. All I knew was that my dad didn't like him and that they never got past whatever was holding them back. "What did he say about the rules, Dad? Did he tell you something about this place?"

"It was crazy, Jared! He told me that we were cursed. Our whole bloodline. That the land the cabin was on had been marked by the first of us that came over from England. He thought we'd left England trying to escape this curse, but that it just followed us, and somehow our ancestors were able to contain it to that property up there."

"A curse?" I repeat, feeling sick as I remember hunting the deer. The silver haze in the air, the hum, the terrifying whispers.

"It's nuts, right? I mean, curses aren't real." My dad huffs out a laugh, and I've never heard him sound quite so unstable as he starts rambling again. "When I was a teenager, he took me out there once and brought me to this flat area with a bunch of stones and showed me how someone carved our family crest in one of them to keep the curse tied to the land. But he said it meant if anyone that wasn't a Loxley by blood or by marriage came there that the curse would go for them. Would make *us* go for them. Hell, he said it happened to him and my mom, but I thought he was just covering for the drinking and the fact that he was an abusive sonuvabitch, I had no reason to—"

"DAD!" I cut him off, trying to process the stream of information that he'd never even hinted at. "Did he tell you what he did to Nana? When they were here?"

"Shit, Jared, that conversation was almost thirty years ago. I just remember him trying to scare the hell out of me so that I wouldn't bring a girl out there, or take my buddies hunting on the property. I thought he was just being a jackass about keeping the cabin and our land private, or that he didn't want me to trash the place with a party. I never believed a word of it."

"It's real," I whisper.

"What?"

"I think it's real, Dad. All of it. There's something here, something evil... It made me do horrible things, Dad." My voice cracks again and I sniff hard, roughly wiping my eyes as I try to grow some balls. "I hurt Harper. I hurt her... a lot. She needs a hospital."

"Christ..." I hear my dad open the car door and slam it, and then I hear the door to the house. "I've got something that will help, I just need to find it."

"Okay." I'm not sure what he could possibly have that will help this nightmare, but when I hear my brother and sister talking to him in the background, I feel even worse. I've never felt so disconnected from them, and I can't imagine ever facing them again. Especially Addison — what the hell could I even say to her?

"Guys, I can't talk right now, I have to do something for Jared. Carrie, can you pack me a bag?" Dad is doing a much better job at sounding calm than I expected, and I feel a little better knowing he's coming out here, but I can hear the strain in my mom's voice as she asks about me. "He's fine, honey. Just needs some help with stuff, so I'm going to go. Don't worry."

"You're coming?" I ask, and I feel like such a kid, needing Dad to come rescue me.

Or put a bullet through my head if I lose my mind again.

"Of course I'm coming, Jared. We have to figure this out. You're on the satellite phone, right?" he asks, and I can hear him digging through stuff, breathing hard into the phone.

"Yeah."

"Okay, well, you need to make sure you charge it. The box is in the closet in the big bedroom." He suddenly sighs, and the sound of flipping pages comes over the line. "I've got it. There's a family up there that helps take care of the property. They keep the fences up, make sure signs stay posted, and my dad always said if anything bad happened out there we could call them."

"Who are they?"

"Their last name is Tuck. I don't think I've talked to them in years, but hopefully Dad wasn't lying about this. Look, I'm going to hang up and call them, but I'll call you right back." He pauses and I think he's going to hang up, but then he mutters a curse and takes a deep breath. "Before I hang up... I need to know what you— what condition Harper is in."

"She's bleeding from her thigh, but I gave her the first aid kit. I don't really know how bad it is, I'm staying away from her. She's got some bruises, and I think she's dehydrated and I..." *raped her. Assaulted her. I'm a fucking monster and you need to kill me before this curse makes me do something else.*

"That's enough. I'll tell them and see what they say. Get the phone charging and stay by it... and stay away from Harper. Understand?"

"Yes, sir," I reply and he hangs up. I know things are never going to be the same again. Not after this — if there is an *after*. I'm still not convinced that putting the gun in my mouth isn't the right decision. If the curse got to me once, then how do I know it won't happen again? I'd rather be dead than put Harper at risk.

Blowing out a breath, I wipe my face off and get the phone plugged in on the floor to charge. As I sit down beside the bed, I suddenly remember taking my phone and charger and putting them under the mattress. Twisting around, I reach between the mattress and box-spring and my fingers brush against something hard. When I pull them out, I clench my jaw against the urge to cry again.

It's all real.

All the memories are real.

I don't know why I was still holding out hope that some part of it could be a nightmare, that maybe I wasn't as terrible as I thought I was... but the phone in my hand proves me wrong. The idea of a curse sounds ridiculous, but it's the only thing that makes sense. I remember trying to fight it, trying to ignore the whispers, but I wasn't strong enough. And was it all the curse? Could it have made me do something I wasn't inherently capable of all on my own? Was I always capable of being this person? A violent, abusive, bastard?

Everything would be easier if I knew the answer to that. My next step, after Harper is safe, would be clear. I'm either forgivable, or utterly damned. I either live or die.

Reaching over to the wall, I plug in my phone to charge, and that's when I remember Harper's phone is still in my pocket, so I push myself off the floor and walk around the bed to plug hers back in. The waiting is the worst part, and I really want a shower, but I'm afraid to leave the bedroom. I don't know what I might do if I see her again. Will I snap again? Is she safe?

The gun.

Without hesitation, I take it out of the holster on my leg and crack the bedroom door just enough to slide it across the floor, then I shut it tight again and return to the satellite phone to wait like I'd promised. I take my mud-caked boots off, tossing my socks after them. My jeans are a muddy mess, but I know I'm filthy and putting on clean clothes right now would just be a waste.

"Jared?" Harper's voice is close to the door, softer, and my heart starts racing.

"Don't come in, Harper. Please."

"You gave me the gun," she says, and I know she's sitting right by the door. So close. I want to open the door and wrap my arms around her. I want to promise her I'll never hurt her again, that I'll spend the rest of my life making this up to her — but I don't have the right to do that. "You're you again... aren't you."

It's not a question, but I'm not sure how to

answer it anyway. "I think so."

"What happened to you? To us?" she asks, and I'm at a loss for how to explain any of it to her. I only just got the information on a possible family curse that goes back for generations, something my dad even *knew* about, but never believed enough to tell me.

"I don't know, Harper. I called my dad, he's trying to contact someone who can help, and—"

"I heard you talking to him. What did he say?"

Shaking my head, I groan as I lean back against the side of the bed. "He said we're cursed. The whole family, or our bloodline anyway." My eyes sting and I press the heels of my hands against them. "This is all my fault, Harper. He told me not to bring anyone out here. He told me *never* to do it, but I didn't take him seriously. I wanted to ask you—" My voice breaks and I slam my fist into my thigh, wanting to tear myself apart for ruining everything. I could have asked her anywhere, I could have asked her at home on the sofa, but no. I had to bring her out here and ruin both of our lives.

"You wanted to ask me to marry you," she

finishes for me.

"Yeah."

"And the curse.... your dad knew about it?" I can hear a subtle tremor in her voice, but I don't know what's causing it now.

"Apparently my grandfather told him about it when he was younger, but he didn't believe him. Which is apparently another tradition in our family. Sons ignoring the warnings of their fathers." I groan under my breath, looking over at the door. "I am so fucking sorry, Harper."

She's silent for a long moment before I hear a quiet, "I believe you."

It's not much, and it's not forgiveness, but I'm so relieved that she's talking to me that I don't even care. "If anything happens, if I do anything weird or dangerous, I want you to kill me. There's six bullets in that pistol, and I want you to use all of them, do you understand?"

"I'm not going to kill you, Jared."

"That... that's not me." I shake my head, remembering the blackouts, the utter loss of control as something flipped a switch in my brain. I'd tried so damn hard to fight it, but it won. "If it happens again, you're not killing me, you're killing whatever evil lives here, and I swear if you don't do it Harper, I'll pull the trigger myself to keep you safe."

"No, Jared, I don't want—"

The satellite phone rings, and I cut her short. "Hold on, my dad is calling back." Answering it, I turn away from the door to focus on my dad. "Hey dad."

"Okay, someone in the Tuck family is a doctor, and they're on their way over with a medical bag and one of his sisters. Somehow they know more about this fucking curse than I do. I'm going to start driving up there right now, but it's going to be about four hours. I don't want you to leave, all right?"

"I understand." I feel like I can finally take a deep breath knowing that someone else will be here soon, someone that will stop me if I start to lose my mind again, because I don't think Harper would pull the trigger.

"Good. Now, I want you to give the phone to Harper. I want to talk to her, but then I want you to get away from her again." My dad is completely in control now. The panicked voice from before is gone, and he's back to his serious conversation voice. I'm worried about what Harper might tell my dad, but it's not like whatever happens I wouldn't deserve it.

"Yes, sir." Pushing off the floor, I carry the phone to the door and lean my forehead against it. "Harper, my dad wants to talk to you. I'm going to pass the phone through the door, okay?"

"Okay," she answers, and as I hand it through the crack our fingers touch for a brief second and I wonder if that's the last chance I'll ever have to feel her skin on mine.

CHAPTER FIFTEEN
Harper

"Harper?" Jared's dad sounds nervous, and I'm curious about how much he knows. Did he know this was possible? Did he do this to Jared's mom?

"I'm here," I finally answer, getting comfortable against the door again.

"First, I want you to know how incredibly sorry I am. I... I don't know what happened out there, but I know Jared hurt you, and I am so sorry, sweetheart. You didn't deserve this, and I take some of the blame for not making sure Jared took the rules seriously. I know my son, and I..." His dad sighs, falling silent for a moment. "I'm not going to make any excuses for him. All I will say is that I know he loves you."

"I know." Turning, I lean my head against the door, listening for him, but I don't even hear him moving around. Part of me hopes he's just on the other side of the door, listening to me. "I know he loves me."

"That's good. I won't ask you to forgive him, or forgive me, but I'm going to ask you to wait there until I get there. There are some family friends on the way, their last name is Tuck, and one of them is a doctor. He's going to look at your leg and help you out, okay?"

"I'm not going anywhere, Mr. Loxley," I say, almost laughing at the idea as I press my hand over the bandage I put on my thigh after I cleaned it. It doesn't hurt nearly as bad as it did earlier though, and I'm not sure if that's just because it's clean or not. "Do you know when the doctor will be here?"

"They told me they'd be there as soon as they could, but I really don't know how close they are to the property, and that road always takes a bit. I'm about four hours away though and I promise I'm going to push the speed limit the whole way." Mr. Loxley takes a deep breath, and I hear him mutter something before his voice returns to the phone. "Be honest with me, are you safe right now?"

"I think so," I answer, and I actually mean it. It sounds crazy, and I know that logically I shouldn't trust Jared at all, or ever again... but logic sort of goes out the window when you watch your boyfriend spew silver fog and then throw up black tar. "Whatever it was... whatever was in him, I think it's gone."

"What do you mean?" he asks, and I know that I haven't spent enough time around Jared's dad to start talking about his son breathing mist and vomiting black sludge.

"It'll be easier to explain in person."

"All right. Well, if you need anything at all, I want you to call me. The Tucks should be there soon and then you'll at least have someone there to help keep you safe." I'm not sure how hard it was for Mr. Loxley to say that, considering the person he wants to keep me safe from is his own son, but it means a lot that he's worried about me.

"Thank you, Mr. Loxley. I... I'm really glad you're going to be here. I think Jared needs you."

"Jesus... Harper, you're something else. I

can't believe you're worrying about him right now, but I love you for it." He lets out a low, bitter chuckle before he takes a slow breath. "You can call me Charlie, and while I don't expect you to do anything after this, I just want you to know how grateful Carrie and I are that you loved our son."

Tears well up in my eyes as I look down at the ring on my hand. It's beautiful, just the kind of ring I'd always imagined I might wear one day, and as I spin it around my finger, I can't lie about what I feel, no matter how crazy it is. "I still love him, Charlie."

"That... that's good, Harper. We'll talk more as soon as I can get there, okay?" Charlie clears his throat, and I smile a little at his gruff voice. "Make sure you get the cord for the phone from Jared so you can keep it charged up. That battery isn't great anymore, and I keep forgetting to replace it."

"I'll do that."

"Okay, I'll see you both soon. Keep yourself safe." Charlie hangs up and I drop the phone into my lap, looking back at the door.

"Were you listening?" I ask, and I'm not

sure why, but I can almost feel him sitting on the other side of the wood.

"You said you still love me," Jared answers, and I hear him sniff.

"It's true."

"No, Harper... no. You can't still love me after all of this, not after... Fuck, I hurt you so bad. I'm never going to forgive myself for what I did to you, I can't even look at you without—" He groans and I feel the thump of his head dropping against the door. "There's no forgiving me. As soon as my Dad gets here, I'll have him take you home. I can go to my parents' house, and I'll move out. You can keep whatever you—"

"Jared, stop." Turning around, I put my hand on the door, looking at the ring that I know he bought weeks or months ago. Long before this trip, before this curse or whatever the fuck it is. "If you remember everything, then you have to remember every time I told you that something was wrong with you, that you weren't acting like yourself."

"Yeah, I remember," he mumbles.

"What you might not remember is having a

seizure on the floor of the living room where a bunch of silvery fog poured out of your mouth like some weird sci-fi movie, and then you started puking up black tar."

"I remember the black stuff."

"Good. Then do you see why I'm inclined to believe all this shit about curses?" I ask, but he doesn't answer me, and I sigh. Taking my hand off the door, I twist the ring on my finger again, pulling it toward my knuckle so that I can look at the circle of shiny, pink skin underneath. The metal actually burned me when he put it on, and I wish he'd let me show it to him. "I think it was the ring that snapped you out of it, Jared."

"That doesn't make sense," he argues, and I roll my eyes.

"As if any of this makes sense? The last few days have been nothing but insanity, and I've been driving *myself* crazy trying to come with a reasonable explanation for any of it — and there isn't one. This is beyond explanation, Jared, but... you came back to me. I saw you freak out, and I'm not sure if you remember all of it, but I can tell you remember some of it."

"If there's more... if I did more to you, I

don't want to know. I already want to die just to make sure I never hurt you again."

"That's not going to happen, Jared." Pushing myself off the floor, I put a little weight on my injured leg and I'm still confused as to why it doesn't hurt much at all anymore. "Open the door."

"No, Harper. I just promised my dad I'd stay away from you, and I'm not going to put you at risk. You stay out there, and I'll stay in here."

I don't even bother arguing with him, I just bang my fist on the door and repeat myself. "Open the damn door, Jared."

"Stop it, Harper!" he shouts, but I can tell it's more from panic than anything else.

"Either open the door or I'm going outside to break a window and climb in, and since my leg is still bleeding a little I probably shouldn't do—" The door cracks open before I can finish the empty threat and I swing it wide, but Jared isn't on the other side. When I step inside, I find him in the far corner of the room, sitting with his knees pulled to his chest, arms crossed atop his knees and his head down. "Jared, look at me."

"Please shut the door again, Harper. I don't want to hurt you. *Please*," he begs, and I can feel the difference in him. This is my Jared, the Jared that I fell in love with, that winked at me and stole my heart in a Philosophy lecture hall. This is the man that bought a ring and wanted to ask me to marry him on what he'd planned to be a romantic weekend. This isn't the monster that wanted to see me in pain, that wanted me scared.

"Look at me and tell me if you want to hurt me." I say the words from the doorway, because although I'm confident, I'm also trying not to be an idiot. It takes a minute for him to finally look up at me, and when he does, he immediately squeezes his eyes shut again.

"Christ, I'm so sorry. I can't believe I—"

"Answer the question, Jared. Do you feel any urge to hurt me? Hunt me down in the woods?"

"No!" He finally looks at me, *really* looks at me, and I can see the pain in his eyes. Normal and green once more, full of life and emotion. "God, I never wanted to hurt you. I wanted us to be together forever. I wanted to *protect* you...

and look at you. I did that to you."

"You really think it was you?" I ask, taking a few steps forward until he raises his hands up.

"Don't. I don't trust myself around you." He looks down at my hands and his jaw clenches tight. "Where the hell is the gun, Harper! Did you really just come in here without it?"

"It's on the floor by the door, but I don't need it, Jared. You may have been somewhere in your head the last few days, but I've been watching you. I probably should have listened to my instincts more, because I could tell you weren't yourself. Hell, I even said it to you, but I kept trying to snap you out of it. I kept hoping if I just helped you, that everything would be okay."

"You need to listen to your instincts right now and get out of here. What if it comes back? What if—"

"Shut up." Sighing, I close the gap between us, even though he tries his best to shove his back through the wall. Shifting to the floor in front of him, I leave an arm's length between us just so he doesn't actually run. "I am listening to my instincts right now, Jared. I love you.

This you, the real you. I don't think all of that supernatural shit would have gone down if it wasn't actually leaving you, and I think if you really focus on how you've felt the last couple of days, you'll realize you feel different now."

He goes silent, his forehead falling against his arms again as he mutters to himself. He's still curled into the corner, defensive, but I know the only person he's trying to protect right now is me.

"Admit it."

"Who cares if I feel different, Harper? I still did"—he waves a hand at my body—"all of that to you."

"If I thought you, the real you, was capable of hurting me like that, I wouldn't be sitting here right now. I would have put a bullet in you the second you slid the gun out the door."

"That would have been the smart choice," he grumbles and all I can do is sigh.

Holding up my left hand, I ask, "When did you buy the ring?"

Jared's gaze lingers on the engagement ring, his brows pulling together as I watch the sadness roll over him. "Two months ago. I kept trying to think of the perfect way to ask you... I carried it with me all the time, just waiting for the right moment."

"And so you decided to bring me to the one place in your life that has been sacred to your family," I fill in, and he groans, covering his face with his hands. Reaching forward, I tug one of them away, holding onto his wrist so he can't hide again. "It was a great idea, babe, and I would have said yes no matter where you asked me."

"I didn't even ask you, Harper. I forced the ring on you just like I forced—" He clenches his eyes shut, his hands balling into fists as he shakes his head. "I don't deserve you after this."

"That's not really your decision, now, is it?" Pulling at his fingers, I make him uncurl his fist so that I can slip my hand in his. "I've wanted to marry you for a while now. I think I've just been assuming it would happen, and you obviously wanted to marry me, or you never would have bought this ring or taken me here to try and make it special."

Squeezing my hand, I can see the emotion raging in his eyes as he stares at the ring. "You're the only one I want, Harper."

"Then I'm yours," I reply, smiling, but then I feel the ring heating up again and I yank my hand back, hissing through my teeth as it scalds my skin. "Shit!"

"What is— FUCK!" Jared stares at his left hand, cringing, and as the heat fades from the ring I shift it out of the way again, only to see an intricate pattern woven in dark ink under my skin right where the ring sits. Jared groans, rubbing at his hand as well. "What the hell?"

"Okay, so... maybe the supernatural shit isn't over," I mutter, moving the ring higher on my finger to show him the mark. When I hold it out, Jared extends his left hand where an identical pattern forms a band on his ring finger.

"This is insane. I actually feel... better?" he says softly, rolling his head from side to side before reaching back with his right hand to run it along the back of his skull. "The knot is gone."

"Are there any voices whispering to you right now?" I ask, definitely feeling more nervous than I did before, but when Jared looks up at me again, I still see *him*.

"No. I don't feel any of it anymore. I felt

kind of hungover before, and my head was pounding."

"That's probably because I tried to bash your skull in with a water bottle," I answer, a smile sneaking over my lips, and he actually chuckles.

"I'm glad you did, we just might need to work on your swing." He smiles and it lights up his entire face, and before I can even think about the risks, I'm leaning forward to pull him into a kiss. Jared goes stiff at first, too tense, but when I slide my hands to the back of his neck, he starts to relax, his tongue tentatively brushing mine before delving deeper, intensifying the kiss for one perfect, sweet moment before he pulls away. "I don't deserve you, Harper. Not at all."

"I'm the only one that gets to decide who deserves me, Jared, and I chose you." Reaching for his hand, I interlace our fingers, not even caring that I'm quoting the cursed version of him. It's the truth. We both chose each other, and he chose me long before the curse tried to destroy us. I shift to lean against the wall beside him, resting my head on his shoulder, and he takes a deep breath.

"I love you so much," he whispers, squeezing my hand tight, and I tilt our hands to look at the mark on his finger.

"I love you too, babe, and I'm pretty sure *your* land just married us, because I'm ninety-percent sure these are tattooed on."

He chuckles again, reaching over to run a finger over the ring created in supernatural ink on his hand. "I think these rings mean it's our land now, Mrs. Loxley."

Grinning, I lean over to press a kiss to his lips. "I like the sound of that."

A loud crash comes from the living room and Jared is on his feet in a second, moving between me and the doorway just as a man steps into it. "They're in here!"

"Is the girl there?" a woman's voice yells, and then she's standing behind the man who's aiming a rifle right at Jared's chest.

"What the hell?" Jared says, raising his hands. "Are you the Tucks?"

"Yes, we are, and you need to step away from the girl Mr. Loxley." The man gestures with the rifle, but Jared doesn't move.

"If you think I'm giving you a clear shot at

my girlfriend, you're insane."

"Actually, I think I'm your wife now, right?" I say, standing up, and I realize my thigh doesn't hurt at all, which is strange, but I'm way more concerned about the man pointing a gun at my... husband? *That feels weird to think.* Moving to stand behind Jared, I try to keep my lower half hidden since he didn't bring my jeans or my underwear back with him, but I feel confident they won't shoot if there's a chance the bullet will go through him and hit me.

"We got a call from Charles Loxley saying his son had activated the curse and that he had a woman here with him in need of medical attention." The man hasn't lowered the gun yet, but I'm not as concerned about him pulling the trigger now.

"That's me." I wave a hand, and the woman steps past him.

"Fran!" he shouts, but she ignores him and grabs my hand, sliding the ring out of the way again.

"Oh thank the Lord," she mumbles, grabbing Jared's left hand to check it as well. "They broke the curse on their own."

"Charles didn't mention that," the man says as he lifts the rifle onto his shoulder.

"Would someone explain what the hell is going on?" Jared asks, and the woman pats his hand with a kind smile.

"I'm Fran Tuck. That's my brother William Tuck," she says, tilting her head toward the portly man in the doorway. "He's a doctor and I think it would be a good idea for him to look you both over, see if you still need any medical attention while we talk."

"That sounds great, I'd just appreciate some clothes first," I say, feeling a blush heat my cheeks as I hold onto Jared's waist to keep him from moving out of the way.

"We'll meet you in the living room," Jared tells them.

"Great. I'll just go ahead and make you two something to eat while Bill gets his things together." Turning around, she waves her hands at him. "Would you put the damn gun away? He's not dangerous anymore."

"How do you know?" Bill snaps, following her into the living room, but we can still hear them clearly.

"Well, if you'd read Papa's journals then you'd know all about the curse and what it took to break it last time. These two have already committed to each other, got the Loxley bands on their fingers and everything. No danger anymore," Fran says in a chipper voice that doesn't seem to really fit the situation. "Well, except for whatever *already* happened to her, and you'll take care of that."

Jared turns around and cups my face in his hands, concern etched into his forehead. "I want you to know that if you want to leave with them, if you want to go, then I won't stop you. I want you to—"

Cutting him off with a quick kiss, I smile. "After all the effort you put in trying to keep me here, would you stop trying to get rid of me?"

"That wasn't me!" Jared sputters as I walk over to my duffel bag and dig out shorts and underwear so that the doctor can still look at my leg.

"Oh, so now you agree with me?" I ask, and he groans, walking over to shield me as I get dressed.

"I just don't want you to ever feel trapped.

Weird magical tattoos or not, okay?" Jared is being serious, and I love him even more for it.

"I'll keep that in mind, babe. But I'm not going anywhere." Buttoning my shorts, I poke his bare stomach and grin. "You should probably put on a shirt so you don't give Fran a heart attack."

"Seriously?" he asks.

"I saw how she was looking at you. She looked like she was ready to track you down in the woods and claim you herself."

Groaning, Jared drops his head back. "This is going to be a thing now, isn't it?"

"Absolutely," I answer, kissing him one more time before I head toward the living room. "After all, no one else has an engagement story like this."

"Harper! You wouldn't!" he shouts after me, and both Fran and Bill look over at the doorway, but he comes out a moment later, tugging on his ratty, worn 'king of the outdoors' shirt, which makes me smile.

I knew he packed it.

"I wouldn't tell anyone, but it's still pretty incredible," I whisper to him and he sighs, pulling me into his side.

"You're the incredible one," Jared says, leaning down to kiss me, and as he parts my lips, I hear Fran's quiet 'aww' in the background.

"These two are cute." Fran's voice floats out of the kitchen and Bill just huffs as he points at the couch.

"What happened to your leg?" he asks me as I take a seat.

"Jared shot me with an arrow."

Bill's eyes go wide, turning to look at Jared who has a similar expression on his face as he raises his hands. "It was the curse. I'm good now."

"Heavens to Betsy," Bill mutters, reaching over to pull the tape off my thigh that I'd looped all the way around trying to keep the bandage in place. "So, when exactly did this happen?"

"Earlier today," I answer, and then I look down at the puckered scar on my thigh. It's still smeared with blood, but when he reaches over with an alcohol swab to clean it away, the wound is completely closed.

"How the fuck?" Jared says, and Fran pops out of the kitchen.

"Language, Mr. Loxley," she chastises, pointing at him before she looks at her brother. "Again, if you'd read Papa's journals then you'd know that once the curse is broken by their commitment to each other, the land heals them."

"Heals us," I repeat, looking over at Bill and then Jared.

"Well, *yes*," Fran says, walking into the living room with a paper towel wadded in her hands. "Why did you think all the Loxleys live so long and stay so healthy?

"My grandfather died when I was seven," Jared argues, and Fran puts a hand on her hip.

"Well, did he stop coming out here?" she asks, and Jared nods slowly. "That's why then. The Loxleys are tied to the land, *this* land specifically. Abandon it for too long and the land abandons you too. When the men come here and hunt, tend the land, the cabin, they renew its force, which is then shared with the whole family." Fran smiles, still sounding way too cheery to be talking about death and magic and curses as if she's reciting a recipe for cookies.

"I need to re-read the journals," Bill mumbles

and Fran laughs.

"You need to read them for the *first* time you mean. Lazy bones." Fran throws the paper towel at him before she heads back into the kitchen, and I look up at Jared to see him lost in thought.

Reaching over, I take his hand and squeeze. "What is it, babe?"

"If she's right... then that means I have to come back here. I have to keep coming back here, back to where I..." he trails off, and I can tell how much he hates the idea, but I pull him onto the couch beside me and squeeze his hand tighter.

"Then you'll come back," I say, trying to sound confident. "You'll need to watch out for Ollie anyway, right? Make sure he doesn't make the same mistakes?"

"But what if we have kids? I'll just have to repeat the cycle, put them and their future loves at risk." Jared groans, and I lean my head on his shoulder.

"You wouldn't be doing it alone, babe. I'll be here," I whisper, and he leans down to capture my lips in a kiss.

"I don't deserve you, but I love you so much, Harper."

"I love you, too," I answer, smiling at him just as Fran comes out of the kitchen again, a bright giggle leaving her as she waves a spatula around.

"Did I hear you two talking about kids? Because if so, there's something else you should know..."

EPILOGUE
Jared

There are days my life doesn't feel real. Harper is beyond beautiful, even more so now than I ever thought she was before, and I'm not sure if it's the fact that she's my wife now, or the perfect little boy she's carrying around in her arms — but I wouldn't trade this life for anything.

Not that it's been easy.

Finishing our senior year at Dartmouth with a baby on the way, and then having a newborn during finals, wasn't exactly how Harper or I ever thought things would go. Then again, I don't think either of us expected to activate a curse that has apparently haunted my family for generations.

We're both determined that what happened to us, and what apparently happened to my grandparents, is never repeated. To make sure, Harper has spent the last year going through every journal in the cabin, and every journal my grandfather kept in his things, to compile an actual set of documents for the rules on being a Loxley. The Tucks have been a huge help, and we discovered through their family history and their Papa's journals that the Tucks, along with several other families, moved from England at the same time. Of course, the *Rules of Being a Loxley* document would probably get us tossed into a loony bin if anyone found it, because it sounds crazy. Curses and magical forests and supernatural wedding bands... if we just had seven dwarves we'd probably have a successful fairy tale on our hands.

Well, an X-rated one at least.

But none of that really matters, because we're together, and I have a real wedding band on my finger to cover up the little pattern that appeared in my skin when Harper chose me. It was my dad that noticed the similarity between the pattern and the old bow in the chest, and none of us think it's a coincidence. There are no coincidences for a Loxley.

We're loved though. So, very loved. Even Harper's parents love me now that they've met Ash. Getting their daughter pregnant and showing up engaged wasn't exactly the best way to join the family, but I'm pretty sure they're over it.

Mostly.

Watching Harper's mom coo over Ash, tickling his feet, has my smile stretching from ear to ear, because there's nothing better than a cute baby to make the in-laws less likely to hang you from a tree. Even if things hadn't gone well with Harper's family, we would have been fine. My dad has been on our side from day one, and I know that he loves Harper all the more for seeing through the tragedy of our family curse. We were just meant to be together.

All of us.

Not just Harper's family and mine, but the extended family that has happily adopted us. I don't know what happened in my grandfather's time that caused a rift between the Loxleys and the Tucks, but we've more than mended it now. Fran has already named herself as one of Ash's aunts, and the whole Tuck family has welcomed Harper and me every time we visit. The Johnsons are on the other side of them, and although they haven't been quite as open to meeting up with us, Fran Tuck is insistent that in time they'll come back into the fold.

Maybe they'll even come to this picnic next year.

A merry band of people united by their connection to me and Harper.

Very few people here actually understand why Harper and I chose this date as our official anniversary, ignoring our actual wedding date completely, but it's the day that means the most to us. It seems impossible that a year ago we were sitting on the floor of the cabin, with me terrified of myself and of a future without her in it. When I close my eyes, I can still see the dirty, bloody mess she was, and I thank whatever powers exist that she still loved me when the curse broke.

That kind of love is rare. Powerful enough to break a curse, and whenever we start to second-guess ourselves, all we have to do is look at the scar on her thigh to remember how close we came to missing all of *this*. The sleepless nights with Ash, the impact to our GPAs, the utter destruction of our social lives... but I know she wouldn't trade it for anything either.

"Your wife is looking for you," my dad says, nudging my shoulder, and I turn around to smile at him before I get up and search the small crowd for her. I find her sitting with Addison, who's holding Ash in her lap, already utterly in love with her nephew.

"Have I been summoned?" I ask, and Harper smiles up at me.

"I wanted a kiss." She grins and I grab her hand, pulling her off the bench and into my arms so I can claim her lips. I love the way she melts against me. I love the way she tastes. I love the little sounds she makes. And, most of all, I love how much she loves me and Ash.

"How did I do?"

"Pretty good, but I know my king of the outdoors can do better," Harper teases, and I roll my eyes and dip her, leaning her head back, so I can completely control the kiss.

One hand fisted in her hair, I nip her lip and

claim her mouth like we're not surrounded by family and friends, the sweet little moan she makes muffled by our lips. When I break the kiss this time, I lean down to whisper in her ear. "Well, my queen, if that's how you want to play, I might just have to fuck you until you beg me to come deep inside you tonight."

"Oh my God," Harper whispers as I lift her upright, earning a few whistles and cheers from our friends as her cheeks turn bright pink.

"Is that a yes?" I ask quietly, and she nods.

"Get a room!" Ollie yells and I turn to point at him.

"Don't make me tell mom and dad about what happened in October," I say, and his eyes go wide.

"What happened in October?" my mom asks as she walks over, and I bust out laughing as Ollie runs for the table of snacks.

"Do you really need to kiss each other like that in front of your *baby*?" Addison asks, bouncing Ash in her lap, and I reach down to scoop him into my arms.

"I think Ash should know how much his parents love each other," I answer, and Harper leans into my side, tickling just under his ear with kisses that make him giggle and coo in the most perfect way.

"I don't think Ash will ever doubt how much we love each other." Harper turns toward me, and I steal another, much more chaste, kiss.

"No way in hell," I whisper as I lean my forehead against hers. "We're forever."

"Screw that," Harper says, and I can hear the laugh in her voice as she wraps an arm around my waist. "We're happily ever after."

THE END

SNEAK PEEK
The Lady

To stay safe in a world she's never known, this lady will pay a steep price...

Adored. Cherished. Pampered. Lady Delilah Darling lives an enviable life. But when cruel hands drive her away from home and into the dangerous streets of London, she's suddenly frightened, vulnerable, and alone. Desperate for safety, Lady Delilah stumbles right into the arms of Henry Gaunt, the irresistible overlord of the London Underground.

Known as The Tramp to his contemporaries, Henry rules his dark world with both charm and violence, bending the willing and breaking all others. Intent on claiming the newly fallen Lady Delilah for his own, Henry offers her protection for a price. Now Delilah is leashed. Claimed. Mastered. And as she accepts her fate as The Tramp's pet, she's left with one question: will she also be loved?

PROLOGUE
The Tramp

Flesh met flesh with a meaty thunk.

A howl of pain.

Blood spurted.

Henry Trampine examined the red liquid, streaking his knuckles, in the flicking, dim light of the tunnels.

Hanging by his arms between two burly men, Cardinal Burr's mouth and nose, poured blood down the front of his chest, dripping over his skin and hair, running in small rivulets to his stomach. His flaccid member hung between his legs, small and shriveled, barely visible under his rounded belly.

"I'm sorry, Tramp," the cardinal gasped. "I'm sorry... I'll get you the money... I will..."

Taller, more broad-shouldered than the average man, when Henry crouched down to the cardinal's level, the other man still had to look up to meet his eyes. Bull and Frank, Henry's left- and right-hand men, kept their tight grip on him. He was no match for either of them, but they never took chances.

It was why Henry considered them his best men.

"I know you will, Cardinal," he replied, his voice low and calm, almost reassuring. The cardinal shuddered. "This is your final warning."

Standing back up, he jerked his head, and Bull and Frank started dragging the man away, still spouting promises. Pulling a rag from the inside of his jacket, Henry wiped the blood off of his hand, his mind already moving on to other things.

Strolling out of the tunnel, Henry barely noticed as people scurried out of his way, averting their eyes when his gaze passed over them. The nobility ruled Mayfair and their estates, and the Prince Regent ruled them, but here in the Warrens, the Tramp was King.

Lady Delilah Darling

"Oh, how lovely," Lady Delilah Darling exclaimed. She lifted her heels and turned, very slowly, on the dressmaker's pedestal, staring delightedly into the mirror. Behind her, Madame Bisset smiled broadly at Delilah before looking at Lady Jane Greene, Delilah's guardian. The older woman's expression was much harder to read, but Delilah was not deterred. She was going to have this walking dress. It was utter perfection.

The rose color set off her coloring perfectly, making her hair appear more fashionably blonde—blondes were more fashionable this Season—her cheeks pinker, and her wide hazel eyes brighter. The trim waist was quite flattering as well, emphasizing her youthful figure. Twisting her hips, the skirts swished around her legs with a gentle shushing sound.

Lady Delilah loved beautiful things.

Moreover, she appreciated them. From the soft, pink fabric of her dress to the pale lacy parasol, she was already planning to use with it to the song of the bird outside the window. Life was beautiful, especially for her. This was her first Season in London, and she was determined to make the most of it as it was likely to be her only Season. Lord Greene had been a fast friend of her late father and had agreed to sponsor her Season, fulfilling her father's final request before his passing. It was the best thing he'd ever done for her. As soon as her mourning period was over, Delilah had made her way to the capital and the Greene's splendid household.

Her father had been a mere baron while Lord Greene was an Earl, but he had taken her in nonetheless as he and her father had been great friends at Cambridge.

She knew the Greene's thought her to be far too spirited, flippant even, but after a year and a half of mourning a father who had barely been part of her life, she truly appreciated all the Season had to offer—the gaudy clothing, the sweaty palms of a nervous gentleman, the glittering throngs. While part of her felt guilty for not mourning her father's death more, it was not as though they had truly known each other. He had spent all of his time in London, leaving her to rusticate at his estate under the care of a nanny, then a governess, and finally, a companion. The companion had been the worst of all, an older woman whose fussy personality had driven Delilah quite mad during her mourning period. She had been very happy indeed to leave the old bat in the country.

The baron had blamed Delilah for her mother's death, though her mother had died of a fever when Delilah was just over a year old. Delilah had caught the fever first, but she had recovered. For some reason, her mother had not. Truthfully, Delilah mourned the mother she'd never known far more than the father who had made it clear he did not want to know her.

Finally spinning around to face her guardian, Delilah clasped her hands in front of her.

"Oh, please, Lady Jane. It is by far the loveliest walking gown I have ever laid eyes on."

Lady Greene's lips pursed, but she was not immune to her young charge's pleas. Ten years older than Delilah, she had so far not been blessed with a child. The second wife of Lord Greene. Rumor had it, he'd married a woman so much younger than himself because he had been desperate for an heir. Ten years later, he still did not have the heir, and gossip said it was likely he never would now, even if Lady Greene were to meet an untimely end, and he was able to marry again. Delilah thought it too bad; the pair would certainly make better parents than her father had.

Even if she was twenty years younger, Lady Greene clearly held her husband in affection, and from all Delilah could see, it was returned. They were certainly happier than most couples among the ton.

They seemed to view their guardianship of her as their chance to be parents, at least in a small way. At nineteen years of age, Delilah was not a child, but her sheltered upbringing and inexperience with Society meant she required guidance, not just chaperones. And if Lady Greene felt inclined to spoil her... well, so much the better. Delilah had blossomed under the Greenes' attention and care, and she was happier than she had ever been in the country. Life was beautiful, exciting, and so very lovely.

"Very well," Lady Greene finally said with a sigh, shaking her head, but her blue eyes sparkled with amusement. Delilah preened happily under her gaze. "But this is the last gown."

Which brought their total for today to ten gowns, rather than the five they had initially planned on purchasing. Over dinner tonight, Lord Greene would shake his head, in much the same manner as his wife, when they confessed their sins, then sigh and hide his own smile before reminiscing about his friendship with Delilah's father. She would listen, but only for Lord Greene's sake. The tales he told did not match her remembrances of the man, but she would not ruin his memories for anything in the world.

"Thank you, thank you, thank you!" Delilah jumped down from the pedestal and threw her arms around Lady Greene. The lady laughed, hugging Delilah back. Delilah always savored such moments. After her nanny had been dismissed when she was five, no one had hugged her again until she came to live with the Greenes. "I am going to be the belle of the park when we go walking!"

"I am sure you shall be," Lady Jane said, still shaking her head and smiling.

The Tramp

Hyde Park—where the beauty of nature was sullied by the grotesqueness of human existence.

Tucked away under the overgrown branches of a willow along the banks of the Serpentine, Henry sneered at the passing ton. Young idiots, prancing about with padded breeches and jackets, posturing like peacocks to impress the simpering young ladies, who cared more about the quality of their purses than their characters. More than one of those young men would be in Warrens tonight, trying their hands at the Tramp's gaming tables.

He wondered what those young ladies would do if they knew the quality of his purse.

He snorted at the thought. Without the title to go with the purse, every last one would turn up their nose at him, no matter that his fortune was as great as any duke. Well, perhaps not all of them would turn up their noses. There were always a few nobles on the brink of ruin. Often enough, the Tramp had helped drive them there. Several had offered their daughters when they ran out of coin—as if he'd want them. The doxies who worked his gambling hells knew their trade, knew how to please a man, and needed nothing more than a room to spread their legs.

Sometimes, he amused himself, wondering if any of those offered daughters eventually made their way to his various establishments. If they did, it was after being broken in elsewhere. Henry did not deal in flesh, other than charging board for the tarts in his hells, and he had no interest in auctioning off young virgins. That was for the brothels to handle.

"'e's not coming," Butch grunted from beside Henry. On Henry's other side, Frank shrugged, but the general air he gave off signaled his agreement.

"Seems not," Henry said, checking his pocket watch again. The Duke of Manchester insisted on meeting in Hyde Park, rather than in the Warrens since he'd promised his new wife he would not step another foot in a gaming hell. Henry actually rather liked the duke, or he'd never have agreed, but he'd also been curious what kind of woman had the formidable man toeing the line so closely. He'd hoped a meeting in the park would allow him a glimpse. "He is a busy man, though. Another quarter of an hour, then we'll leave."

Butch nodded, and Frank shrugged again. It wasn't as if it was a hardship to spend some time in the park, other than the obnoxious occupants. But the weather was fair, the air even cooler by the river, and it certainly smelled better than the Warrens.

Scanning his gaze back across the river, he saw her—a vision in pink and cream.

Henry hated pink. He wanted to rip the offending gown off of her delicately curved body and tear it to shreds. The impulse shocked him. He enjoyed women. He reveled in their whimpers, moans, their pained and pleasured screams—but he'd never had such a visceral reaction to any other member of the female persuasion. He could not have even said why she was so different. But she was. His body reacted, his pulse beating faster, cock hardening, fingers twitching to get his hands on that abominable dress... and her. He could strip her, pull off that ridiculous bonnet, and keep her clothed in nothing but her hair, like Lady Godiva. With her hair covered up, he could not even tell what color it was, but it didn't matter. Whatever color, it would be better than that dress.

Those sweet pink lips curved in a smile, and Henry had the urge to ruin those as well. He'd kiss her until her lips were red, pinch her nipples until they matched, and spank her sweet cunt to the same color before fucking her into oblivion. He'd keep her naked, well-spanked, and well fucked—his little pet…

The vision was so encompassing, he did not even notice time passing until Butch cleared his throat again.

"Uh, Boss? We gonna keep waitin'?"

Jolted from his reverie, Henry pulled out his pocket watch. It had been another half hour, not a quarter. Growling, he cast one last look across the water at the woman who had clouded his mind—a bloody debutante. Standing in the park for so long must be making him barmy.

"Let's go," he growled, turning his back and stalking away. Bloody debs. Bloody women.

But he already knew he'd be ordering whatever whore he used tonight to dress in pink.

GRAB IT NOW ON AMAZON

ABOUT
the author

Cassandra Faye lives in Texas where she's done nothing but fantasize about other worlds her entire life. Constantly daydreaming about ancient powers, faerie realms, old gods, and how seriously dangerous unicorns would be if they existed, Cassandra writes the stories she's always craved. Taking paranormal and fantasy worlds, mixing them in with modern day, and adding a dash of darkness.

So, if you enjoy those fairy tales that were a little more *grimm*, or if you ever wondered just how bad the villains could be as you held on for that happily-ever-after, then you might be just the person she's writing for.

https://www.fayebooks.com/

Don't miss a release! Sign up for the newsletter to get new book alerts at:
https://www.fayebooks.com/newsletter

Cassandra also writes dark contemporary romance as Jennifer Bene. You can find her online throughout social media with username @jbeneauthor and on her website:
www.jenniferbene.com

ALSO BY
the author

Daughters of Eltera Series (Dark Fantasy Romance)
Fae *(Daughters of Eltera Book 1)*
Tara *(Daughters of Eltera Book 2)*

Standalone Dark Fantasy Romance
Hunted *(The Dirty Heroes Collection Book 13)*
One Crazy Bite

The Thalia Series (Dark Romance)
Security Binds Her *(Thalia Book 1)*
Striking a Balance *(Thalia Book 2)*
Salvaged by Love *(Thalia Book 3)*
Tying the Knot *(Thalia Book 4)*
The Thalia Series: The Complete Collection

The Beth Series (Dark Romance)
Breaking Beth *(Beth Book 1)*

Fragile Ties Series (Dark Romance)
Destruction *(Fragile Ties Book 1)*
Inheritance *(Fragile Ties Book 2)*
Redemption *(Fragile Ties Book 3)*

Dangerous Games Series (Dark Mafia Romance)
Early Sins *(A Dangerous Games Prequel)*
Lethal Sin *(Dangerous Games Book 1)*

Standalone Dark Romance
Imperfect Monster
Corrupt Desires
The Rite
Deviant Attraction: A Dark and Dirty Collection
Reign of Ruin
Mesmer
Jasmine
Crazy Broken Love
The Institute: A Dark Anthology

Standalone BDSM Ménage Romance
The Invitation
Reunited

Standalone Suspense / Horror
Burned: An Inferno World Novella
Scorched: A New Beginning

Appearances in the Black Light Series (BDSM Romance)
Black Light: Exposed *(Black Light Series Book 2)*
Black Light: Valentine Roulette *(Black Light Series Book 3)*
Black Light: Roulette Redux *(Black Light Series Book 7)*
Black Light: Celebrity Roulette *(Black Light Series Book 12)*
Black Light: Charmed *(Black Light Series Book 15)*
Black Light: Roulette War *(Black Light Series Book 16)*
Black Light: The Beginning *(Black Light Series Book 17.5)*

Made in the USA
Middletown, DE
20 November 2023